INTERCEPTED

ALEATHA ROMIG

NEW YORK TIMES BESTSELLING AUTHOR

The Coopers Series Book One

By New York Times bestselling author Aleatha Romig

business drama, corporate intrigue, forbidden, star quarter-back, strong heroine, billionaire romance

SACKED - Coopers book three - Coming July 2026

SCORED - Coopers book four - Coming September 2026

RECENT RELEASES

RUSHED - Coopers book two - April 2026

INTERCEPTED - Coopers book one - February 2026

NAUGHTY AND NICE - A Brutal Vows Holiday Novella

- November 2025

Marriage of convenience, Mafia/cartel romance, romantic suspense, friends to lovers, he falls first, strong heroine, possessive hero, dangerous romance

FEAR OF FLAMES - A Romantic Thriller - October 2025

*Suspense, Crime, Corruption, Protective hero, Strong heroine, Thriller, Mystery, Romance, Curvy heroine, dangerous romance *Stand-alone*

DEFENDING LOVE - Standalone Novel

A steamy, high-stakes, romantic suspense with body-

*guard vibes, second chances, and all the feels—set in the same world as the Sinclair Duet *Stand-alone*

TO HAVE AND TO HOLD - Brutal Vows, book five - March 2025

Arranged marriage, Mafia/cartel, enemies to lovers, age-gap, he falls first, protective hero, Romeo and Juliet vibes, dangerous romance

QUEENS AND MONSTERS - Brutal Vows, book four - January 2025

Arranged marriage, Mafia/cartel, alpha hero, virgin heroine, touch her and die, family saga, he falls first, possessive hero, sheltered heroine, dangerous romance

BOUND BY A PROMISE – Brutal Vows, book three - October 2024

Arranged marriage, age-gap, forbidden, Mafia/cartel dangerous stand-alone romance

ONE STRING – July 2024

Aleatha's Lighter Ones - Second-chance, enemies-to-lovers, fake-date, little-sister's-best-friend, forbidden, stand-alone contemporary romance

TILL DEATH DO US PART- Brutal Vows, book two - June 2024

Arranged marriage, enemies to lovers, Mafia/cartel, he falls first, stand-alone, dangerous romance

NOW AND FOREVER – Brutal Vows, book one - May 2024

Arranged marriage, age-gap, Mafia/cartel stand-alone romance

For a complete list of all Aleatha Romig's works, turn to BOOKS BY ALEATHA at the end of this novel.

Cooper:

A skilled craftsperson who makes or repairs wooden barrels, casks, and tubs.

DEDICATION AND INSPIRATION

To my husband who continues to support me, sliding food under the door as I barricade myself in our office and spend time with my imaginary friends. Also, for my family, our love of football and particularly the Indianapolis Colts, who have given us great memories and unforgettable moments. Whether we're all in the same room or spread across the country, we are all together at kickoff. This shared affection as well as the Colts franchise in particular are my inspirations for the Coopers series. Thank you. I love you all!

SYNOPSIS:

In *The Coopers*, family power meets forbidden passion, and one wrong move can cost you the team... or your heart. Perfect for fans of the ruthless tension of *Succession* and the dark, aching obsession of *Wuthering Heights*.

At thirty-six, Fin Graham is a legend—a veteran quarterback, dangerously handsome, and built to win. The field. The season. *Me.*

I never thought I'd see him again, not after he disappeared and shattered me without a word. But now he's been traded onto my family's team, the Lexington Coopers—*my* turf, *my* legacy, and the one place I swore he'd never touch.

No one knows our past.

No one knows how hard I loved him... or how deep the betrayal cut.

And if I have any sway with the team's owner—my

father—Fin's contract will be the shortest in franchise history.

But the problem with old heartbreaks?

They remember how to start beating again.

Fin wants a second chance.

I want revenge... or maybe I just want him.

And the time clock is almost out.

With the future of the Lexington Coopers on the line, we have to decide if we're working together or against one another.

From the bestselling author of *Infidelity* and *Sin* comes a scorching, high-stakes romantic suspense series set in the seductive, cutthroat world of the NFL. *The Coopers* is a four-book saga following one explosive couple. INTERCEPTED ends on a cliffhanger—an unforgettable Aleatha blindside.

CHAPTER 1

Vee

The impending unease that came with our upcoming gathering ran through my circulation. It wasn't a business meeting that we were about to attend, and yet it was. The Hubbard family suite. My nerves were on edge as I took in the crowd. A sea of amber surrounded Crystal Light Stadium.

Energy crackled through the warm air as fans wearing their Coopers gear made their way inside. While this afternoon was the second game of the preseason for the Lexington Coopers, it was our first home game. Attending this game became a family tradition long before I, Maeve Hubbard, was born over three decades ago. To hear my father talk, I was only a tiny baby when I attended my first Coopers game all decked out in Coopers amber.

Not attending this event was impossible.

When I was a child, my paternal grandfather, Carroll Hubbard, owned the Lexington Coopers. Today, that title went to my father, Reid Hubbard, the official owner and CEO of the NFL team. Lifting this season's excitement to a feverish pitch, the oddsmakers had the Coopers named for the AFC championship and a contender in next February's Super Bowl.

A security guard nodded and opened the door to the private entrance. Preston, my boyfriend, laid his hand in the small of my back, directing me toward the massive entryway and private elevator, the one that would whisk us up to the suite level. As we came to a stop before the elevators, I took a step away from Preston's touch. In truth, I wasn't a fan of public displays of affection, especially not at Crystal Light Stadium, where I was so easily recognized.

His deep voice resonated through me as his grin quirked and he whispered, "Don't be sassy."

Preston was a handsome man and heir to Kentucky thoroughbred royalty. While my family lived and breathed football, Preston's family was all about horse racing. My lips curled as I looked up into his shining dark-brown eyes. "If you think that was sassy, you've underestimated me."

"Vee-eee." He elongated my name as his smile waned. "Time got away from me last night. It's nothing to hold a grudge about."

Pressing my lips together, I shook my head.

"Miss Maeve," Jim, the familiar usher at the elevator, said with a smile, saving me from my conversation. "Your father will be happy to see you made it."

"I wouldn't miss this game for the world." I couldn't help but return Jim's infectious grin. He was as much a part of the Coopers' history as my family. I couldn't recall a time he wasn't present. Offering him my hand, I said, "Jim, welcome back. It's good to see you."

He took my hand and gave it a firm shake. "It's sure good to see you, Miss Maeve. Did you know that this is my twenty-ninth season?" he asked, his neck straightening with pride.

"I didn't. Wow. We need you. It wouldn't be the same without you."

"I'm not going anywhere." His grin grew. "You were just a little thing when I started working here. I sure do miss Mr. Carroll, but it does my heart good to see the Hubbards and Marshes carrying on the tradition."

The elevator arrived with a ding, barely audible with the growing crowd noise around us. The doors opened and two ushers I didn't recognize came out.

Jim held the doors open. "Take my station" —he said to the other ushers— "while I take Miss Hubbard and her guest up to the family suite."

They both nodded their heads. "Miss Hubbard, welcome."

As I stepped forward, Preston's hand again went to my back. Before he made full contact, I met his stare. Pressing my lips together, I barely shook my head. I wasn't upset about last night. It was a surprising relief when he'd spent more time during our friend's party with the men in the basement bar than upstairs with me. "Stop," I mouthed.

Preston's smile evaporated and his jaw clenched as he took a step away.

It was that realization of enjoying his absence that had me reeling.

Once inside the elevator, Jim swiped his credentials over the sensor, commanding the elevator to bypass the other floors and whisk us directly to the top level.

Staring at the shiny doors, I saw my boyfriend's reflection over my shoulder. My thoughts went back to Preston's recent request. A little less than a week ago, he asked me to move in with him. For a couple in their mid-thirties who'd been dating for over two years, cohabitation was the natural next step. It wasn't unusual for one of us to spend the night or weekend at the other's place. Yet his invitation didn't give me joy. Instead, it somehow felt suffocating, the thought causing my skin to feel unnaturally tight.

I'd told him I needed to think about it.

After last night, I wondered if it was space that I sought instead of cohabitation.

If Jim noticed any of Preston's and my nonverbal battling, he didn't let on. Instead, he continued his charismatic role. "Six-hundred suite level," he announced as the elevator came to a stop.

"Thank you, Jim," Preston and I said in unison.

This was the top level and the location of the two most luxurious suites in the stadium. About twelve years ago, my father investigated moving the Coopers to another city. The negotiations were truly a game of three-dimensional chess involving city officials, fans, and the team. As I recalled, the Lexington fans were overwhelmingly supportive of the team staying put and building a new stadium. We officially moved into Crystal Light Stadium eight years ago.

In 1978, my grandfather purchased the team, including the old stadium, for $20 million. Compared to today's standards, that building was outdated and small.

Dad and his brother-in-law, Darin Marsh, spent months touring stadiums and practice facilities around the country. They saw the best locker rooms, playing fields, spectator seating, medical rooms, and office space. As the blueprints materialized, it became clear that Dad wanted not only those spaces but also a family suite, not a generic hospitality suite that was available to others for a price. The result was that whether Crystal Light Stadium, owned by the Coopers, was the venue hosting another NFL team or the sight of a concert, our family had a place we could call home. And the space was as much our collective family's as the living room in the twelve-bedroom cabin near Gatlinburg, Tennessee.

Preston leaned near my ear. "It would be nice if Jim would refer to me as Preston or Mr. Clark instead of Miss Maeve's guest."

My cheeks rose. "Oh, I'll be sure to talk to him about that right away."

Preston and I continued side by side until we arrived at the Hubbard Family Suite. Those words were written on the placard beside the entry. A female usher was stationed outside the door with an iPad in her grasp.

Preston reached for my arm, turning me to him. "Vee, I don't want your family to think we're fighting."

His wide chest was in my line of vision. I stared at the front of his amber polo shirt. A bourbon barrel, the Coopers logo, was embroidered over his left pectoral muscles. My gaze lifted, meeting his narrowed stare. "Are we fighting?"

He lowered his voice, seemingly undeterred by the usher and spoke through clenched teeth. "I don't know what the fuck this is." He motioned toward the door. "I know your whole damn clan is either inside there or will be soon." He widened his eyes. "Is this about my invitation to move in with me?"

Multiple responses went through my mind. I settled on the truth. "I've been thinking about it."

"Then stop."

"Stop?"

"Maeve, I'm not trying to rush you. I just thought it made sense. I mean we're usually at my place or yours. If it's the location, I could just as easily move in with you."

Move in with me?

Is that what I want?

I took a deep breath and feigned a smile. "Can we maybe not talk about it today?"

Preston nodded.

When we turned, my cousin Leigh and her husband, Hayden, stepped from the same elevator we'd recently exited.

"Oh, hi." Once they were near, I leaned close and gave Leigh a hug. The two of us were the same age, each other's best friend, and the closest either of us had to a sister.

"Hi," she said with a smile as Hayden and Preston shook hands. "What's the big discussion about?"

"We have a bet," I said. "I think Daphne won and she's had the suite refurnished with golden thrones. Preston thinks the thrones are only at their house."

Leigh quirked her smile. "I call bullshit."

Shaking my head, I rolled my eyes.

Leigh looped her arm through mine. "Oh, we're going to need to chat."

The usher by the door wore a name tag that read *Trina*. As the four of us approached, she smiled. "I'm sorry. I need your names, please."

"Maeve Hubbard and Preston Clark," I replied.

"Hayden and Leigh Quinn," Hayden said.

Trina reached for the door handle. "Enjoy the game."

The view as we entered was as awe inspiring as it had always been. The large space was designed like a living room, including multiple large-screen televisions, a firepit, and of course, the bar and buffet. Beyond the room, separated by open glass doors, was a long counter with twenty-six tall stools overlooking the end zone. Farther out and down a few steps were twenty-six reclining chairs that felt as though they were hovering near the end of the playing field.

With today's summer-like temperatures and blue skies, the retractable roof was open, bathing the field and some of the recliners in sunlight.

"Vee," my father called. "Grab a drink. Darin and I want to talk with you."

Leigh looked at me and grimaced. "Good luck with that."

CHAPTER 2

Vee

When Preston claimed my clan would be present, he was correct. The suite was filled with familiar faces. Uncle Darin was waiting with my dad. He was the husband of my aunt, my dad's sister, Rachel. After Grandpa Carroll's death, Dad named Uncle Darin co-vice president of football operations, a title he held in conjunction with his wife. Grandpa Carroll left the team plus half of his estate to Dad. The other half of his estate went to his daughter, Aunt Rachel. Before Grandpa's death, Dad and Aunt Rachel were co-vice presidents until Grandpa named Dad CEO.

The Coopers franchise was the family business. Two of my cousins, Grant and Phillip, and I were employed by the team. The only family member to step away from the Coopers was Leigh, who chose to become a lawyer. While she currently worked for the state defender's office, Dad and Uncle Darin were actively campaigning for her to move away from public defending and set her sights on corporate law, specifically working for the Lexington Coopers.

Lip sent me a grin and a wink. As cousins, Lip, Leigh, and I were always close. Being five years older than us, Grant thought he was too mature to hang with us. Some would think that would change with time, but even today that age-difference chasm still existed, among other divides.

I didn't think about Preston as I made my way toward the bar.

My stepmother was seated at a barstool with a gin and Diet Coke—her game-day tradition. Daphne Hubbard had a flair for drama. My dad and she married when I was in middle school. While she was ten years younger than my father, now with treatments that cost my father a fortune, she appeared closer to my age. As I approached, I noticed that today she had a mix of brown and amber lowlights in her long blond hair. Daphne was also wearing the Coopers amber. However, licensed apparel wasn't her thing. No, she wore a flowy amber blouse, four-inch-heeled gold sandals, and tight white capris accented with gold jewelry.

I forced a smile. "Hey, Daphne."

"Hi, Vee, glad you could make it." She leaned back and scanned me up and down before pressing her lips together disapprovingly. "You look comfortable."

My lips curled as I took her in. To say our relationship was like a mother and daughter would be inaccurate. As a preteen girl, I wasn't exactly thrilled with a new stepmother and made my opinion known.

Through the years, we'd learned to coexist. Even with our truce, our styles were different. Instead of high heels and flowing garments, I was more comfortable in blue jean capris, a Coopers t-shirt, and a pair of crocs. "Oh, thanks. That was the look I was going for." I lowered my voice. "Do you know what Dad wants to talk to me about?"

Brent, the waiter behind the bar, came forward. "Miss Vee, would you like a cosmo?"

I shook my head. "I think I'll stick with Diet Coke today."

He smiled. "Late night?"

"Me?" I asked with feigned shock.

"Diet Coke coming up."

Daphne responded to my question. "Darin and your dad are discussing a quarterback. He's a veteran, been in the league for years. Royce signed him to a one-year contract. He's going to play today's game." She shrugged. "You know how it works. If they decide that he's not worth the money, he'll be off the roster and on the practice team before the preseason ends."

"And Dad wants to talk to me about him?"

She took a sip of her drink and nodded. "Your dad thinks you know him."

My forehead wrinkled in question. "Who would I know that he doesn't?"

"Oh, Reid knows him. It's that Fin played for University of Kentucky while you were a student. You had that internship with the team." She stirred her drink with the straw. "I think he only played at Kentucky for a short time. Then he went to Tennessee. Your dad's curious about your thoughts."

While I heard the first part of Daphne's answer, the rest was lost to the growing static in my head. Fin. Griffin Graham. I was a sophomore at Kentucky, and he was a redshirt sophomore despite the two years he played at Kentucky State, a Division II school.

"Vee?"

I shook my head and began to reach for my Diet Coke. Instead, I lifted Daphne's glass and took a hearty gulp. The gin tingled on my tongue and throat. Warmth filled my cheeks as I met her gaze and lowered the glass. "Oops."

Taking back her glass, she offered, "Brent can add some gin to your glass."

I picked up the cool tumbler of Diet Coke. "I think I better stay sober for this discussion."

Her eyebrows rose. "You know Mr. Graham?"

"I did. But honestly, it's been almost fifteen years. I'm sure my knowledge won't be helpful."

My heart sank as I looked up, seeing that Royce Beasley, the Coopers' general manager, was now standing with Dad and Uncle Darin out by the tall counters at the top of the outdoor seating area. Mr. Beasley had been around since before my dad became owner over twenty years ago. In other words, he was older than dirt and wasn't much into asking the opinion of others, especially those of us—Aunt Rachel and me—without a Y chromosome.

A quick glance found Preston with a beer in his hand, sitting on the half-round sofa near the gas firepit, talking with Hayden and Lip. I steeled my shoulders and approached the three men beyond the open glass doors. Sunlight filtered through the opened roof, giving the sensation of walking outdoors. In reality, it was outside. In January, when the snow could be falling, this area would be a warm and comfortable seventy degrees. With the retractable roof closed, it would also be inside.

Dad lifted his arm, resting it over my shoulders.

"Hey, sweetie, your uncle Darin and I have a question for you."

My position with the Coopers was vice president of stadium operations and marketing. With my BA in sports management and an MBA, I anticipated that when I came to the Coopers, I was fully prepared. It turned out that while an education was nice and the degree looked impressive on the office wall, it was no substitute for getting dirty in the trenches. Over the last eight years, I'd learned more from my coworkers and assistants than I ever learned in a classroom. For the record, stadium operations and marketing had nothing to do with football operations, Aunt Rachel, Uncle Darin, and Royce Beasley's side of the Coopers. In other words, as a VP, I had no say in which coaches or players the Coopers drafted, signed, fired, or interviewed.

With a smile pasted on my face, I asked, "What's your question?"

Uncle Darin turned toward me with a light beer in his grasp. "Do you remember a player named Griffin Graham from when you were at Kentucky?"

"He goes by Fin," Royce said.

"That name sounds familiar," I replied, keeping my voice from giving away any emotion. "My internship didn't start until my junior year. I think he had transferred by then." I shrugged. "I don't know where he went." That was a lie.

"Tennessee," Dad said. "Graham's had a successful career. He was a second-round draft pick by Atlanta where he played out his rookie contract. Other than his rookie contract and six years with Green Bay, he's moved around a lot."

I scrunched my nose. "He's getting old, isn't he?" I knew his age, two years older than I—his time in Division II. Mentioning his age was subjective. A thirty-six-year-old man was hardly old as in geriatric. However, for football, he was approaching the end of his career.

Royce laughed. "At seventy-four, I'm old. Fin has aged like a fine wine."

"Why are you asking?" I asked. "Is there a problem with Dennison?" The Coopers acquired Troy Dennison in last year's draft. He was a first-round draft pick and a rookie from Alabama. Last year, he'd taken us to the AFC championship. We'd extended his four-year contract and tripled his salary.

"Dennison is good," Dad said. "And Simpson is still strong. We're discussing a third-string quarterback. The other teams will be gunning for Dennison after last year. We need reliable backups."

I stifled a laugh, recalling Fin's ambition for greatness. "You want to sign Fin as a third string?"

"Or second," Royce said with a shrug. "We'll see how the boy plays. I've been watching him this last week at practice. He used to play with Downing"—he turned to me—"our first-string tight end, when they were both at Green Bay."

My fake smile returned. I wanted to interrupt Royce and inform him that I was aware who Downing was, and I could name the rest of the team and their positions if he wanted, with the obvious exception of a recent hire. Sometimes, it was exhausting wanting the respect others received so effortlessly.

We turned as Uncle Darin's son and my cousin Grant joined our conversation. "Are you telling Vee about Fin?"

I met my cousin's gaze. "Seems everyone knew about his hire except me."

"But you know him, right? Lip and I were trying to remember. Didn't you date him?"

His question was a kidney punch. "Who did you date in college, Grant? Do you remember every one of their names?" Grant was a confirmed bachelor. Given his position with the Coopers, my cousin was probably one of Kentucky's most eligible bachelors.

Grant's lips quirked. There was a twinkle in his eyes. "Define *date*."

"See, I remember Griffin Graham. Dating?" I pursed my lips. "I don't think that happened."

Dad tapped my shoulder. "We can talk about this later. It's about time for the national anthem."

I smiled and looked out on the field. There were nearly one hundred high-school football players unfurling a mammoth flag that would dominate from twenty-yard line to twenty-yard line. I'd been the one who worked with the different athletic offices to arrange these students' opportunity to be on the national stage.

As the crowd cheered, Leigh came up behind me. "Can I steal you away?"

I spun, my smile blooming. "Please and thank you."

CHAPTER 3

Vee

Fourteen Years Ago

The house off Burley Avenue reeked of stale beer, marijuana, and sweat. I moved my feet, my sandals sticking to the kitchen floor from the runoff of the keg. Or maybe it was from spills, no one seeming overly stable. Every square inch was occupied, people standing against walls while others sat on the dirty sofas and even on the questionable carpeting. During my one trip to the bathroom—which was disgusting—I saw bedroom doors open and others closed. Scanning the faces, there were few I recognized. The music blaring from hidden speakers and shaking the walls made my temples pound. I was half expecting the Lexington police to be the next guests through the door.

With my wildcat t-shirt sticking to my skin and perspiration dripping down my back and between my boobs, I reevaluated my current life choice. Emma, my roommate, had spent the better part of last week talking about a great off-campus party, one we couldn't miss. She'd been told about it in her economics lecture.

Honestly, that should have been the first red flag. It wasn't like economics majors were known for their epic parties. The sheer number of cars required us to park multiple blocks away.

Swiping loose tendrils of hair away from my face, I shook my head at Emma. "Let's get out of here," I shout-whispered.

"I want to stay and see if Aaron makes it." Her large blue eyes were open wide. "He was the one who told me about the party. He even asked me on Friday if I'd be here."

Friend code meant that if Emma stayed, I stayed.

"Fine. I'm going outside. I can't breathe in here."

Emma reached for my hand. "Don't leave, Vee."

"I won't. You either."

She nodded as I turned in the direction of the front door. A quick assessment let me know that I couldn't forge a possible path through the crowd of bodies.

Instead, I headed toward the glass doors off the living room, in the other direction.

The door was open, mixing the outside heat with a sad attempt at air conditioning. Looking beyond the windows, I saw that since we'd arrived, the sun had made its descent. The sky wasn't quite night, but also, no longer day. One light on the side of the house illuminated the cement patio. Stepping out, I took a deep breath, trying to fill my lungs with fresher air.

A group of guys sitting around a resin table turned in my direction. "Hey, sweetheart," one in a blue UK shirt said, his words slightly slurred.

"Hey." I sidestepped the table, heading out into what was supposed to be a back lawn.

"If you're looking for a place to sit?"

I turned to see that the blue shirt had pushed himself back, offering me his lap. "No thanks."

My response got laughs and comments from blue shirt's friends.

"If you change your mind—"

"There you are, Abby," a deep voice called from the dimness beyond the bubble of light. "I was afraid you'd left." The holder of the voice materialized—tall, muscular, with short dark hair, a sharp, chiseled jaw, and eyes whose color I couldn't define. He came to my side and spoke to the table. "Tell me which one of you assholes was making a play for my girl, and I'll kick your ass."

Everyone else at the table laughed and pointed to blue shirt.

Blue shirt stood, albeit wobbly. "Seriously, Fin. I didn't know."

The mysterious Fin turned, looking down at me. "It's up to you. Do I kick Sean's ass?"

I took a moment to consider my answer. "I think you should let him off this time."

Fin pointed at Sean. "You heard the lady. She saved your ass this time. She won't be around to do it the next time."

Sean lifted his hands in surrender and retook his seat.

Fin and I turned away from the table and began to walk through the backyard. "Abby?" I asked.

His cheeks rose. "Abby or Emma. I swear every girl in every class has one of those names. Sorry, are you Emma?"

"That's my roommate." I worked to conceal my smile. "Two strikes. One more and you're out."

We'd come to a side street. Across the street was a park. The sign read Burley Park. I lifted my face to the summer breeze, taking in the fresh air.

Fin stopped and offered me his hand. "I don't want to be out, so I'll try this. Hi, I'm Fin Graham."

I laid my hand in his, a spark of sensation coming to life within me. "Hi, Fin Graham. I'm Maeve Hubbard."

We released one another's hands.

"Maeve." He hummed my name. "I should have known you were too unique to be an Abby or an Emma."

"Most people just call me Vee."

"Fin is short for Griffin. Only my grandma calls me that."

"Fin it is then. Thanks for coming to my rescue. Honestly, I'm pretty sure I could have taken Sean. It's being outnumbered that I didn't appreciate."

The sky grew a darker shade as we continued walking into the park, my shoulder rubbing against his arm.

"I don't doubt you could kick Sean's ass," he said. "I would have been happy to do it, but that could have fucked up my scholarship." He smiled. "It would have been worth it."

I bumped against his arm. "And I thought chivalry was dead. Tell me about your scholarship."

Time lost meaning as we sat, the two of us, on a park bench just outside the globe of a tall streetlight and talked. During that conversation, Fin asked if I knew anything about football.

Starting a conversation with 'my dad owns an NFL team' wasn't my go-to. Instead, I nodded. "I know some. My major is sports management. I've volunteered with the athletic trainers to help with water for the team."

"A water girl."

"A water *person*," I corrected. "I'm hoping that next year I'll get an internship with the football team, working with the trainers."

"We may have a problem."

"A problem?"

"Sean and those other assholes at that table…"

I was listening.

"They're on the football team. So am I."

My eyes opened wide. "You are? I guess without the jersey…"

Fin shook his head. "You wouldn't remember me. I'm a transfer this year. I played two years at Kentucky State."

"Division II." I'd heard about this new quarterback. "Are you the redshirt I heard people talking about?"

"That would be me. I'm a junior in credits, a sophomore on the team."

"I'm a sophomore in credits." I recalled what he'd said earlier. "What's our problem?"

"I just told that table you're my girl."

"Oh," I said with a laugh. "And that my name is Abby."

"Those assholes won't remember your name. However, they'll remember you when they see you on the field. You're too pretty to forget."

Warmth filled my cheeks. "So should we tell them we had a big fight over them and now it's over?"

Fin reached for my hand.

His touch was warm and secure.

"I'd rather we stick with our story." He tilted his head. "Unless there's someone else. I mean, I could kick his ass."

I shook my head. "No one else. Besides, we don't want to jeopardize your scholarship."

"See, my girl is looking out for me already."

As my phone in my back pocket began to vibrate, I pulled it out. The name on the screen read *Emma*. "I need to get this. It's my roommate. She's back at the party." I hit the green icon. "Emma?"

"Where are you?"

"I'm not far." My forehead creased. "Are you okay?"

"I'm out front. Aaron finally arrived with a blond bimbo on his arm."

"Ugh. I'm sorry. Stay there. I'll be there in a couple of minutes."

"Vee, I want to get out of here. Tonight was a disaster."

"Be right there," I said, disconnecting the call while at the same time, certain she was wrong about tonight's assessment.

"Is that our cue?" Fin asked. "You need to go?"

"Yeah, friend code. Emma wants to leave."

Fin turned his hand palm up. "Can I see your phone for a second?"

A warm tingling fluttered through my nervous

system as I handed him my phone. Fin took it and turned away. When he turned back, his smile was even larger than before. "I just sent myself a text. Now we have one another's numbers."

I retrieved my phone and stood. "It will make it easier to continue our charade."

Fin stood, his wide chest before me. Craning my neck, I looked up. Under the streetlight I could see his eyes were blue, a striking shade reminding me of sapphires.

"I was thinking maybe we could see one another again, not on the football field."

My lips pressed into a straight line. "I suppose I do owe you for saving me."

"Nope. Talking to you was the best part of this night. I only went to that party because the team would be there. I'm no saint, but I'd rather not get caught with alcohol and weed before my first game as a wildcat."

"The only beer I got was what's stuck to my shoes."

Fin laughed as together we walked back to the party house.

CHAPTER 4

Vee

Present time

"What was really going on in the hallway with you and Preston when Hayden and I got here?" My cousin widened her green stare and lifted her barely visible eyebrows —the ones that matched her light blond hair. "You haven't talked to him since we arrived."

Leigh and I were standing in a corner with a large screen to my back. The national anthem rang throughout the suite. Not answering her question, I turned to the screen. The singer was a local artist who

Preston and I heard singing at a wine festival last autumn. She had the perfect voice for our fans. I followed up. She was elated. I also know she was nervous. I held my breath as she elongated the word *free*, her voice going up an octave or two. And next came the word *brave*. The entire stadium erupted in applause. "Great pitch."

"Yeah, she's great."

I scanned the room before turning back to my cousin who wore an expectant expression. "I'm not ready for these weekly family gatherings."

Leigh looked at Daphne, now hanging on my father's shoulder. "You know, I'm surprised they're still married."

A laugh bubbled from my lips. "I was thinking the same thing." My smile dimmed as I shook my head, my thoughts going back to Preston's and my discussion before entering. "It's nothing. I'm just..." As I tried to formulate an answer, my gaze went behind Leigh to Preston's profile. He was undoubtedly handsome, and when it came to conversations, he was a master captivator. It was probably his family's old money. There was an innate confidence in him. As he spoke, people hung on his every word. "Look at him," I whispered. "He doesn't need me at his side. He can work the entire room."

"Oh, I know what's happening."

It was my turn to lift my brows; however, mine were

dark like my long hair and more visible. "What do you think is happening?"

"You're at that two-year itch."

"What two-year itch?" I asked.

Leigh pressed her lips together and brought her finger to her chin. "Let's do a rundown. How long did you and Kelcee last?"

An uncomfortable warmth caused my temperature to rise. "I don't remember. Besides, he wanted to move to LA. He got that offer from the Rams."

"He asked you to move with him."

"And leave Lexington?" I asked aghast. "Leave the Coopers and all our family fun?"

"As I recall, he offered a long-distance relationship, and you said no."

"Those don't work."

"All right," she said, "how about Josh? He was fun."

"Too fun." I pursed my lips. "With too many women."

"Yeah, Josh doesn't count. I wanted you to break up with him sooner than you did. Oh, what about Noah?"

Noah was fun to be around until he wasn't. I shook my head. "Your point?"

"My point is you and Preston have been together for about two years, and that's your breaking point. You find a reason to break things off."

Nibbling my lip, I looked again at Preston. His head

was back in a dramatic laugh. "He asked me to move in with him."

"Oh my God," Leigh said overdramatically as she clenched her hands over her chest. "He obviously doesn't know you. I'm surprised you didn't break it off right then. I can't believe you brought him to the game."

"Are you saying I have commitment issues?"

"Girlfriend, you are the poster child for commitment issues."

Before I could give that more thought, the suite erupted in cheers and applause.

Leigh and I took a step back, turning to the large screen.

Touchdown Coopers scrolled across the screen.

"Holy shit," Uncle Darin screamed. "Anyone who didn't see that pass, watch the replay."

"Number seventeen?" Leigh asked as the camera showed the formation from behind. "Graham." She was talking about the quarterback. Another camera zoomed in on his face.

I sucked in a breath at Fin's blue stare. His concentration was intense as he called the play. His deep voice echoed in the large stadium. The ball was snapped at the Dolphins' twenty-yard line. Despite knowing the outcome, my heart fluttered with the palpitations that accompanied watching our team.

Fin received the ball. He stepped back, his eyes

scanning the field as the Coopers dispersed into formation. Back and forth he danced, his footwork only improved from our days at Kentucky. A Dolphins defender came close. Fin didn't flinch as our offensive player pushed him back.

Fin's arm went back. He released the ball; it spiraled through the air over the heads of the Dolphin defense. Tight end JD Downing picked the ball from the air near the Coopers' thirty-yard line and tucked it safely against his body. It seemed as though none of the defenders anticipated that long of a pass. JD was all by himself as he sprinted into the end zone.

"Well, shit," I mumbled.

"Shit?" Leigh asked as she jumped up and down. "That was fantastic. Who the hell is Graham?"

"If he keeps this up, he'll be our number-one backup quarterback," Lip said, coming to where Leigh and I were standing. He nudged me with his elbow. "Damn, just like when he played for Kentucky, right, Vee?"

"Someone tell me who this guy is," Leigh asked again.

To my surprise the voice at my side was Preston's. "Griffin Graham." His arm encircled my waist, pulling me toward him. "Who I just learned is an old beau of Vee's."

Craning my neck, our eyes met. "He's not—"

"Griffin..." I turned back. My cousin had that faraway look. Then her eyes met mine. "Shit. Fin?"

I straightened my neck and shoulders. "Yeah, it's Fin. We haven't spoken in nearly fifteen years. Nevertheless, my opinion is that he's too old. One good hit and he'd be out for the season."

"Vee," my father said, coming closer with a smile on his face. "Did you watch that amazing pass? Royce was right about Fin and JD. I could watch that replay for hours."

I obviously had my work cut out for me to convince the men in this suite that Griffin Graham was not a good fit for the Lexington Coopers. "He's probably icing his arm as we speak."

Preston's warm breath tickled my neck as he leaned closer. "You never told me about him."

I spun out of his grasp and met his stare. "There's nothing to tell." My teeth were clenched together. "We went to college together for one year. I honestly haven't thought about him for a decade."

Before Preston could respond, I turned away, walking to the bar. It was silly for me to be defensive about Fin. I hadn't thought about him recently. Ten years would be a stretch. Reading the weekly stats, his name jumped from the page. I didn't want to follow his career, but I had. After he played his rookie contract for Atlanta, one season for the Buccaneers, and six years at Green Bay, he went to LA and his name disappeared. I assumed he was in retirement. The last thing I expected was to see him in a Coopers uniform.

Exhaling, I appreciated that no one followed me. The barstools were empty. I scanned the room for Daphne. She and Aunt Rachel were sitting at the counter beyond the glass doors, watching the game live.

"Miss Maeve, another Diet Coke?" Brent asked.

"I'm ready for that cosmo."

A smile and a nod, and Brent went to prepare my drink.

My gaze went up to the screen. It was near the end of the first quarter. The Coopers were up, seven to three. As I started to think about our defense, I lifted the glass to my lips. Leigh appeared back at my side. Taking the barstool to my side, she lowered her voice. "Did you know about Fin? Is that why you're having second thoughts about Preston?"

My lips puckered as I swallowed. "I didn't have any idea about Fin until we arrived." I remembered what Uncle Darin said. "And according to Royce, he's been on the roster for an entire week." An insincere smile curled my lips. "It's not like the people in football operations make a point in keeping me informed."

"If you told Uncle Reid that you didn't think Fin was a good hire, do you think he'd listen?"

"Maybe if I knew before today. After that throw and touchdown..." I shook my head. "Besides, breaking my heart doesn't dispute the fact that the man has talent." I took another drink, my mind replaying memories I thought were dead and buried. "I hope he's icing his arm."

"How old is he?"

"Thirty-six," I answered without hesitation.

"Maybe if you tell Uncle Reid what happened between the two of you..." She looked hopeful.

I inhaled. "It was a long time ago. My damaged ego shouldn't stop his career." I twisted my shoulders as the cosmo's vodka surged through my bloodstream. "Besides, Royce said he's looking at him for third string. Not exactly the illustrious career Fin intended."

"Lip just said second string." She looked up and pressed her palms together as if in prayer. "Not that I want anything to happen to Troy Dennison, but second string is only an injury away from first string."

"Troy Dennison is more than a decade younger than Fin. My money is on Troy."

CHAPTER 5

Vee

A view of the amber shade carpet met me as I entered the Maker's Mark Football Center. This was the official training facility and office complex for the Lexington Coopers, roughly twenty miles west of Crystal Light Stadium. On Monday morning, the practice fields were dark. The players were meeting with their coaches to evaluate film from Sunday's game.

This state-of-the-art facility contained football operations offices, business offices, meeting rooms, and classrooms. We had an indoor and outdoor practice field. There was a large locker room, a weight room with the newest equipment, a training and rehabilitation area, and even a hydrotherapy room. A large kitchen and eating area supported our team's nutrition program.

At the same time, Crystal Light Stadium was in the process of transforming from a football stadium to the host of a three-day medical sales conference and trade show. The event would bring over fifty thousand people to Lexington, showcasing the versatility of the stadium. This was something Dad and Uncle Darin promised as incentive for our new stadium.

While the locker room, weight room, and practice field were mostly empty this morning, behind the scenes, the Coopers' personnel were busy. Our trainers were busy helping injured players heal and deciding which players if any would be added to the injury report.

The coaches were already in the viewing room reviewing film from the game against the Dolphins with the players. I'd sat in at many of their meetings. Roy Everington, who coached the Coopers for five years, welcomed me into their tightknit circle. As the only child of the owner, my future would forever include the Coopers. I wanted to know all I could.

While Tilson, the current head coach, wasn't as accommodating, he didn't mind when I went to him with questions. Nevertheless, my experience with

Everington taught me that Mondays were critical days. The coaches broke down the game, analyzing every play, every failure, and every success. Whether it was offense, defense, or special teams, there were hours of video to analyze. As it turned out, the Coopers lost yesterday's game thirty-three to thirty-four.

While our offense was strong with Fin and a few appearances from Simpson, our kicker missed two extra points and hit two field goals, one from fifty-seven yards. I didn't envy the coaches trying to dissect that mess of stats.

"Preseason isn't about winning and losing," Grandpa Carroll used to say. "It's about finding the right combination to do better than before."

That was his motto—improving. Always improving.

The empty practice field reassured me that I would have less of a chance to end up with an impromptu meeting with our newest signed player. Breathing a sigh of relief, I waved to the receptionists near the entrance and made my way to my office within the area of stadium operations. Bestowing the title of vice president on me was another step in preparing me for what will happen when Dad was gone.

That's not a subject I lingered on. My father was sixty-five on his last birthday. While the future of my personal life was unsure, professionally, Dad would be around to teach me, Grant, and Lip what the next generation needed to know.

"Good morning, Vee," Jen, my assistant, said as I entered the business offices. "Do you need anything before the morning meeting?"

"Good morning." I smiled at her bourbon barrel earrings. "Those are cute."

"I bought them in the gift shop before the game yesterday."

I nodded. "I think I'm good. I'm going to check my emails to be sure my ticket information is correct. Then I'll be on my way."

Not long after I sat down at my desk, there was a knock on the door. Dad peeked his head inside. "Oh good. You're here."

"Dad, come on in." I looked at my watch. I was later than normal, but not late. "Our meeting isn't until ten?"

My father took his position as CEO and president seriously, but at the same time, he didn't believe in stuffiness. He wanted a casual environment of teamwork. His button-down shirt, blue jeans, and leather loafers fit that image. Despite his age, Dad was a handsome man with thick salt-and-pepper hair, a fit body, and vibrant green eyes that matched my own. "I wanted to talk to you alone before the executive meeting."

The two cups of coffee I'd already consumed percolated in my stomach. "Okay." I stood, smoothed my tan skirt, and motioned to the comfortable seating area near floor-to-ceiling windows that looked out over the outside practice field. "Do you want to sit?"

Dad nodded. Once we were both seated, he asked, "Is there something you want to tell me about Griffin Graham?"

Pressing my lips together, I considered my answer. Despite the ache in my chest, I shook my head. "I can't think of anything."

The fissures at the side of Dad's eyes deepened. "Grant mentioned that the two of you have a history."

Another shake of my head as I exhaled and offered a bare-bones answer. "I knew Fin at the University of Kentucky. We went out a few times. He was offered a deal to transfer to Tennessee. The Vols at that time were an NCAA top-ten team. It was a better university to showcase his talents. Fin took the offer, and that was it."

Dad nodded. "Tennessee helped make Graham a second-round draft pick. Atlanta drafted him."

"I didn't follow his career." That wasn't completely accurate. I followed him through Tennessee, Atlanta, and on to Tampa Bay. After that, even though I told myself I didn't care, I still followed his stats.

"Royce wants him even more than he did before.

After yesterday, he wants to renegotiate Graham's contract."

"Renegotiate? How?"

Dad leaned back and lifted his ankle to his knee. "Fin's agent agreed to the original one-year contract. After yesterday, Graham put himself on the radar of other teams. It wouldn't be that big of a loss to him if he chose to let one of those teams buy out his contract with us. Royce thinks we need to offer more."

I nodded, despite my inner turmoil at the prospect of Fin being part of the Coopers into the future. "This is why I'm not involved with football operations. Royce is good at finding talent."

"We've talked about it before. You need to spend more time in football operations. Let Grant show you how that side of the franchise works."

"Grant?"

"Vee, one day you'll be in my position. The Coopers is a business. That's the way every decision must be approached. Ask yourself, what's best for this season? And then ask, what's best for the future of the team? If those answers contradict each other, then it's time to find new answers."

"Do you think Mr. Graham is good for the season or for the future of the Coopers?"

Dad exhaled, his nostrils flaring. "Season. As you said yesterday, his age is a factor."

"Then I don't understand why we would renegotiate his contract. Does Royce think Fin has three years in him?" When Dad didn't answer, I leaned forward. "Grandpa also said the Coopers was about people. I crunch numbers. Sometimes what's best for the numbers isn't best for our people."

Dad's smile grew. "This afternoon, Royce and I are meeting with Fin and his agent. I'd like you to come with us to that meeting. I've also invited Grant."

It wasn't as if I would turn down my father's invitation. However, I wished he would have left the part about Grant out of it. "Grant." My lips pressed together.

"You two will be working together in the future. Grant is essential in communication; he also has a good mind for the football side of the business. Vee, you're more like your grandfather. You have the heart of the Coopers as your main concern." He smiled. "Rachel is like you, too." He took a deep breath and lowered his ankle. "She confided in me yesterday that she's ready to retire after this season. Darin wants another year or two, but that timeline would mean that we'll need you, Grant, and Lip moving up sooner than previously discussed. Will your increased responsibilities be a problem?"

"No."

"What about you and Preston?"

I stood, my hands slapping my thighs. "How exactly is my personal relationship a factor?" Before he could answer, I asked, "Did you pose the same question to Grant and Lip?"

"They aren't seriously dating anyone to my knowledge."

Lip was dating, but that wasn't my place to announce it. "Dad, I don't know what's happening between me and Preston. He invited me to move in with him and" —I inhaled— "I don't think I want that."

"Then don't do it."

He made it sound so easy. "Leigh says I have commitment issues."

Dad stood and took a step toward me. "I disagree."

I hadn't expected this conversation to go so personal; nonetheless, I wanted to hear my father's point of view. "You don't? ...Think I have commitment issues?"

"No, Maeve, you're committed to this family and the Coopers. When the right person earns the privilege to be part of that commitment, you'll know. If it's not Preston, then it's not him."

"I'll be at the ten o'clock a.m. meeting and attend the one with Fin and his agent. I doubt he even remembers me." I scoffed. "Grant admitted he doesn't recall everyone he went out with in college."

"If Griffin Graham doesn't remember you, I'd hesitate to offer him a more lucrative contract. No matter how well he can throw a ball, I'd question his cognitive abilities to remember plays because my daughter is unforgettable."

My cheeks rose. "Thanks, Dad. It doesn't matter what he remembers. If you, Uncle Darin, and Royce think the Coopers will be better with Fin Graham, I'm behind you. Personally, I want to keep Dennison healthy. And what the hell was happening yesterday with Holt?"

Dad shook his head. "I'm certain that's a discussion with the special teams' coaches. Do we concentrate on the fifty-seven-yard field goal or the two missed points after?"

"Grandpa always said it's not about winning or losing. It's about improving."

"Sometimes, I'd like to walk into the office and find him sitting behind my desk. I'd ask for his advice."

I walked with Dad toward the door. "I'm glad I still have you to talk with."

He winked. "Don't worry. Despite Daphne's pleas, retirement isn't on my short list."

"She wants you to retire?"

"It's not happening."

After Dad left my office, I went to my desk and collapsed onto the white leather chair. I'd told myself that today was a free pass. With the players in meetings all day, that meant I had zero percent chance of running into Fin. That likelihood just went up—way up. It was time to put on my big-girl panties and be the woman I'd become—Maeve Hubbard, vice president of the Lexington Coopers. No longer was I a smitten twenty-year-old girl.

My thoughts briefly went to Preston.

Was Dad right?

Was my commitment issue more about what I was committing to than my ability to commit to anything or anyone?

CHAPTER 6

Vee

"Calls and online sales for tickets tripled yesterday," I reported to the people around the table, "and the trend is continuing as we speak. Season tickets have been sold out since last March. The available seats are getting snapped up. There's a good chance that every home season game will be a sellout."

"I still think we should consider expanding the stadium," Grant said.

Dad lifted his hand. "We've discussed that. Crystal Light Stadium is only eight years old. Only Las Vegas has a newer facility. Ours holds over seventy thousand fans. It's the fourth largest stadium with a retractable roof. Instead of discussing expanding the relatively new facility, let's talk about how to make each fan's experience better so they want to renew next year and the year after. The way to do that is to have a winning team."

Grant pressed his lips together and tapped the end of his pen against the table. It wasn't the first time Dad had put a stop to his idea of expansion. Even a sideways glance to his dad, Uncle Darin, did nothing to propel the discussion.

"Vee?" Royce said, looking my direction. "Reid said you're going to be spending more time with football operations this season."

I swallowed, my gaze going to Dad.

"We talked about it earlier," he said.

"What did you have in mind?" I asked Royce.

"Grant thinks it would be good for you to attend practices, learn the play calls and the formations."

I turned to my cousin. "Why?"

"Because there's more to the Coopers than ticket sales and scheduling half-time entertainment."

"Let me talk to the coaches. We'll get something worked out," Royce said.

Uncle Darin changed the subject. "It should be common knowledge by now that we signed Griffin Graham to a one-year contract."

The reminder of our upcoming meeting caused my pulse to accelerate. Sometime during the night, I'd convinced myself that Fin could play for the Coopers without any interaction from me. That notion was obviously ill-founded.

Dad was speaking. "...Beasley, Darin, Grant, Vee, and I are meeting with Mr. Graham and his agent this afternoon to discuss extending that contract."

Questions came from around the table. Dad replied as he had to me—Fin's performance on Sunday was spectacular. The Coopers didn't want to risk Fin being lured away by another team.

"Do you want to grab some lunch before the meeting with Graham?" Dad asked after our meeting ended.

"I brought something from home," I said. "What time is the meeting?"

"One o'clock in the Carroll meeting room."

I feigned a smile. "I'll see you then."

I hadn't brought food from home, but I wanted a few minutes alone to prepare myself before meeting Fin's sexy blue stare for the first time in nearly fifteen years. I'd been only twenty when we first met, that fated night at a horrible party. That was fourteen years ago. We'd said our so-longs less than a year later. It wasn't supposed to be goodbye.

Life interrupted both of us and the plans we had.

And here we were.

Those were my thoughts as I made my way toward my office. My two-inch pumps made no sound on the amber carpeting. My gaze went upward. Along the tall hallway, banners with the likeness of each current player hung. A smile tugged at my lips at the picture of Troy Dennison. He would keep the quarterback position and Fin would fade away. He'd get tired of playing backup and move on to a team that could use him.

Entering the business offices, Jen came toward me. "Did you get my text?" she asked.

"No." I shook my head. "I had the volume off. Sorry, what did I miss?"

"Griffin Graham is here to see you."

My circulation rushed to my feet, making it difficult to remain standing. "He's here?"

She nodded, her eyes wide. "In your office." She lowered her voice. "He's a lot taller than he looked on the jumbotron. And his eyes..." She inhaled.

I didn't need to hear her assessment. I knew every word she said was accurate. "Did he say why he wanted to see me?"

Jen shook her head. "He asked if you were in today. I said yes, but you were at a meeting. He introduced himself and asked if he could wait for you." She shrugged. "That's all I know."

Damn. I should have eaten lunch with Dad.

"Thanks, Jen. I have a meeting at one. Could you give me a call in fifteen, an excuse to end the meeting with Mr. Graham?"

"I can do that."

Inhaling, I straightened my neck and shoulders. My suddenly sensitive breasts pressed against my white silk sleeveless blouse as a cold chill scattered over my flesh. I looked down, mentally demanding my nipples not to bead. It was my body's response to the memories of a man, not the man behind the door. One more glance...I hoped that if my body betrayed me, at least my padded bra would do its damn job.

Exhaling a calming breath, I lifted my chin and pushed open the door to my office.

While I thought I was prepared to meet with Fin face-to-face, I wasn't. Seeing him again in person after so many years was closer to the materialization of memories, ones I'd buried deep inside, than to reality.

As I entered my office, Fin stood, his eyes opening wide. He'd been seated where Dad had been hours earlier. Wearing dark blue trousers, a button-up shirt open at the collar, and shiny leather loafers, he could easily be on the cover of GQ.

For a moment, we remained silent, each one scanning the other. I wished I could have ascertained that in the last fifteen years Griffin Graham had developed a beer belly, a face-altering injury, or even wrinkles due to excess sun.

None of that was true.

Fin was even sexier than I remembered, causing my core to twist and my nipples to harden. I didn't look but silently prayed my bra was doing its job. Obviously, my body hadn't followed my command.

The youth of Fin's and my first meeting morphed into maturity that couldn't be categorized by years alone. The world we once shared split in a cosmic divide, taking each of us on separate journeys that somehow had once again collided.

The hint of gray in his dark hair gave Fin character. His chiseled jaw had grown sharper with time, the edge covered by merely a shadow of hair. Beneath his expensive clothes, I could tell that his body had matured, yet judging by his wide shoulders and trim waist, I could see he'd remained toned as only an athlete could. The intensity of his sapphire blue eyes brought back an ache I hadn't experienced in years.

Refusing to show the cauldron of emotions bubbling to life within me, I pressed my lips together. "Mr. Graham."

His lips quirked. "Abby, I wanted to talk to you."

Abby.

He remembered our first meeting.

My cheeks fought to rise, yet I held them resolute. I offered him my hand. "Mr. Graham, in case you didn't know, I'm Maeve, Maeve Hubbard."

He stepped forward, taking my hand in his, his long fingers swallowing mine as warmth transferred from him to me. He held on longer than was socially acceptable. As I pulled my hand free, the tips of his lips curled, revealing a blindingly white smile. "I do remember. You go by Vee. And I go by Fin."

Trying unsuccessfully to quiet the rush of circulation in my ears, I turned and walked toward my desk. Once my tablet and papers were on the hard surface, I straightened my shoulders and turned back to my guest. Motioning to the chairs, I managed to speak. "Please, let's get this over with."

"Vee," he said, still standing, his hands resting casually at his sides. "I don't want things to be awkward or uncomfortable around here."

Pressing my lips together, I shook my head. "I'm vice president of stadium operations and marketing. I have little to no interaction with the players." Although that seemed to be shifting.

"That's too bad," he said, taking a step toward me.

Without thought, my gaze went to his left hand. What was I doing? There was no reason for me to speculate. Surely, there was a wedding band. Had I heard of him marrying? I hadn't thought of that until this minute.

Fin must have followed my gaze because he lifted his left hand and wiggled his fingers. The only ring was a smart ring he wore on his first finger. "Not married."

"Not my concern."

His timbre unexpectedly ricocheted through me as

his deep baritone voice carried through the air. "Are you or have you been?"

"Not your concern."

"I was," he shared, his tone self-abashing. "It only lasted less than a year. I think she had some preconceived notions about being married to a professional football player. I didn't fulfill those expectations."

I set my jaw, and pressing my lips together, I inhaled. "Mr. Graham, we're about to meet with you and your agent, my father, uncle, cousin, and Royce Beasley to discuss your contract. Any discussion regarding personal information is inappropriate."

He took a step closer. "I told you about the failed marriage because to be honest, I'm not good at relationships. It isn't anything new. I made some horrible choices when I was younger, a lot younger."

"Can I take that to mean you won't fulfill your contract?"

"No." He opened his eyes and clenched his jaw. "I will uphold my end of the contract."

I crossed my arms over my breasts. "Tell me, Mr. Graham, why did you agree to come to the Coopers? You had to know I would be here."

"Would you believe me if I told you that your presence with the team weighed heavily on my decision to come to Lexington?"

"Honestly, no. I don't believe you."

CHAPTER 7

Vee

Nearly fourteen years ago

My soprano laugh combined with Fin's baritone scoff as our sounds filled my bedroom.

"You think it's funny?" he asked, his muscled body pinning me down to the mattress.

Looking up at his handsome face, I grinned. "I think you had female professors at Kentucky State, and you sweet-talked your way into higher grades. Professor Williamson is eighty years old and a man skeptical of athletes. No flattery will influence his grades."

Fin peppered my neck with kisses. I writhed beneath him as it both tickled and sent goosebumps over my skin.

"Stop," I squealed.

He stopped, his nose meeting mine. "I'll have you know I aced intermediate economics and statistics at Kentucky State with both male and female professors. Managerial economics with Williamson is as boring as listening to Sean talk about girls. A *D* won't get me kicked off the team, but it doesn't look great for a transfer portal."

My smile dimmed.

The air had just been sucked out of the room.

"What's the matter, Vee?"

Shaking my head, I pushed and rolled out from under his bulk. Sitting on the edge of my bed, I straightened my sweatshirt. "I thought you didn't want to transfer?"

Fin was now next to me, his legs manspread, with one blue-jean-clad thigh next to mine. "I don't."

I turned, meeting his gaze. "Fin, don't lie to me. I know the Wildcats aren't having the best season, but it's been better than last year. With you on the team, it will be even better next year."

"I only have two more years of eligibility in college ball to make a name for myself. My dad..." He pressed his lips together. "Nothing's set. Forget I mentioned it." He gently elbowed my side. "I'd take some extra tutoring in managerial economics, and I happen to know this fantastic girl who's acing the class."

It was difficult not to melt when he smiled, and his eyes seemed to see only me. "So the truth comes out. You're only dating me for my help with classes."

Fin's large palm cupped my cheek, pulling my face toward his. "Your brilliant mind is only one of the reasons."

As our lips touched, my circulation accelerated, twisting my need deep in my core. The conversation was gone; a warm buzzing filled my ears as our tongues teased and taunted. Fin tasted of coffee with a hint of mint. My senses were on overdrive, from the taste of toothpaste to the spicy scent of his bodywash. With the first man to ignite my passion, I was running blind into a level of relationship I'd never known.

Each minute we spent together since the horrible party four months ago intensified my desire. I wanted things I had never really considered with anyone else.

Breaking free, I scooted onto Fin's lap, straddling his legs, and pressing my breasts against his hard chest. His fingers splayed beneath my sweatshirt on my lower back. I rubbed my sensitive core over the hardness forming beneath his blue jeans.

He tugged my sweatshirt over my head, causing our lips to separate. His smile curled as he stared down at my breasts, pushing the limits of my bra. A skillful twist of his fingers and the clasp was released, the straps falling from my shoulders, and a chill scattered over my flesh at being exposed. Fin tossed the bra to the growing pile of clothes on the floor and lowered his lips, finding and teasing my hardened nipples. Licks, nips, and sucks caused my breasts to ache with the heaviness that only he'd provoked.

Lifting me, Fin stood.

My ankles locked behind his waist as he took a few steps. The cold wall against my shoulder blades alerted me to our location. I opened my eyes, meeting his stare. My body and mind were at war, a fierce battle raged between what I thought I wanted with Fin and how far I was ready to go. Words seemed to be jumbled as I struggled with what to say. "I-I..."

"You're beautiful, Vee." His thumb caressed my cheek, and the pad ran over my lower lip. "Your lips are swollen" —his smile grew— "because of me."

He dropped my legs, my tiptoes reaching the floor. Remembering what he'd said earlier, I pushed against his chest. My gaze met his. "Are you planning to leave Kentucky, to transfer somewhere else?"

Fin's smile dimmed as he took a step back. "I don't know."

I shook my head. "How the hell don't you know?"

He reached for my hand. "I don't want to leave you."

"It's not about me. It's about your future." Pushing around him, I reached for my sweatshirt now lying on the floor and pulled it over my head. "Thanksgiving break is coming."

Fin nodded.

"I'm staying in Lexington." I wanted to invite him to come along, yet inviting someone with football dreams to visit the owner of the Lexington Coopers was scarier than it sounded. There was the little voice in my head that said, 'he's not interested in you, only in your family.' As it was, Fin had never mentioned knowing the connection, and I'd never told him that my family owned an NFL team. I'd only said my last name was Hubbard, and I was from Lexington.

"I'm going to Bowling Green."

Swallowing back the emotions, I straightened my shoulders. "It's going to be boring. My dad and Daphne will be out of town."

"Come to Bowling Green."

I shook my head. "I can't do that."

His handsome features softened. "It's only a long weekend." He spun around, lifting his arms over his head. The muscles in his biceps bulged beneath the band of his t-shirt. "Is there someone else waiting for you at home? Someone you want to see other than your parents. Is that why you won't let us go further than we've gone?"

How far we'd gone.

I'd gone further with Fin than I had with anyone else.

To his credit, Fin was remarkably patient. We were three months into our relationship before I let him touch me below the waist. As it was, I'd come on his hand. Maybe it was the football, but Fin had an ability to create a rhythm that ignited fireworks while leaving me breathless and wanting more. It was during the fourth month that I ventured below his waist. He'd been campaigning for oral, but that hadn't happened yet.

"No," I answered truthfully, not someone as in a boyfriend.

"Then come with me to Bowling Green. I've told my mom all about you."

My anger at his last question subsided. I hadn't told anyone about Fin except my cousins Leigh and Lip. My response came slow, the words separated by space. "You told your mom?"

He lowered his arms. "I did." A lopsided smile formed. "She wants to meet you."

I tipped my chin toward my chest and inhaled. Looking back up, I felt the need to explain. "I'm not a tease, Fin. I think I'm scared."

"Of what?"

"Of you. Of us. That you might like me for another reason."

He took a step closer and lifted his touch to my hair. "Is there a wrong reason to like you?" Before I could answer, he went on, "I like you for your brain.

You're not just book smart. You're fun to talk to. I don't have to explain football. Hell, you know the game better than half the team. You don't sugarcoat things for me. When I fuck up, you don't just tell me, you talk to me about ways to improve. And as for book smart, I was hoping you'd help me prepare for my econ final." His touch lowered, over my shoulders and down my arms. "And if that wasn't enough, you're also beautiful. No, stunning. I especially like you when you're like you are now, hair down, cheeks pink, and lips swollen" — his smile grew— "or how you were a few minutes ago, without that sweatshirt. But damn, when you dressed up like you did for the banquet, you blew me away. You're like model gorgeous." He ran his hand over his hair. "I've never met anyone like you. Other girls are..." His Adam's apple bobbed. "They aren't you, Abby."

A tear threatened to escape my eyes.

Abby was Fin's code word, one no one else would understand. If he was uncomfortable with a situation, such as during practice, he'd call me Abby with a wink. It meant that he was watching. The other players knew to keep back because I was Fin's.

"Hello." Emma's voice came through my closed bedroom door. "I wanted you to know I was home. No sex in the living room."

I looked up at Fin. "Living room is off-limits."

"Oral is off-limits?"

I nodded. "Not forever. Maybe we should study

managerial economics. We need to get your grade up"
—I took a breath— "for the transfer portal."

"Vee..."

I lifted my finger to his strong full lips. "Fin, I'm not selfish. I want you to pursue your dreams. I'll support you even if it means we're across the country from one another. I also want oral with you. I want more with you."

"Living room sex?"

My grin returned. "Maybe one day. Right now, all I ask is that you're honest."

"I can do that."

CHAPTER 8

Vee

Present time

My rebuttal hung in the air.

"I deserve that," Fin said, his smile fading. "I'd like to start fresh here with the Coopers. To be completely honest with you, Vee, it was—"

Hearing my name from his lips affected me like fingernails on a chalkboard. "Maeve or Ms. Hubbard," I interrupted, "would be more appropriate going forward."

Fin inhaled, his nostrils flaring. "Ms. Hubbard, as I was about to say, it was JD, the Coopers' tight end—"

Shaking my head, I interrupted again, "I'm aware of all the players on our team. Please don't be so condescending as to assume you need to tell me the positions of our players."

"My apologies, Ms. Hubbard. As you are probably aware, JD and I played together in Green Bay. I'm certain you also know that players talk. JD sang the praises of the Coopers' organization. I have a few more good years in me. I'd like to play for a franchise that appreciates all members of the team."

"Troy Dennison will take us to the Super Bowl."

Fin's smile returned. "And as his backup, I'll have a front-row seat to his magic. He's a talented kid. I'm not disputing that."

We still hadn't taken our seats. "I recall a man who didn't want to settle for second place or third," I added.

"I was the starting quarterback for two seasons in Atlanta, one in Tampa Bay, and five in Green Bay. Maybe I've finally decided that being plowed down by the defensive line is something I'm willing to let the younger studs do on a daily basis. However, if I'm needed, I know I can perform. The Coopers are a stronger team with me on the roster."

A scoff escaped my lips as I dropped my arms and shook my head. "There's the Griffin Graham I recall. Always so confident or should I say cocky."

"You have me wrong. I accepted the opportunity to sign with the Coopers because my goals in life are changing." He narrowed the distance between us to only a step or two. His cobalt stare was laser focused on me. "I want more out of life than football. It's taken me a long fucking time to realize that, too long. I asked you if you were married, but I know the answer. I know that you're currently seeing the douchebag Preston Clark."

"This isn't—" I began to protest.

"Maybe it's the Clarks' old money you're after, but I never took you for a gold digger."

"I don't need anyone's money. Preston is..." I tried to finish the sentence, but my mind was suddenly void of complimentary adjectives.

Fin's smile widened. "That tells me all I need to know."

Before I registered what he was doing, Fin had my hand in his, and he bowed at the waist. His lips brushed my knuckles. When he stood erect, there was a gleam in his gaze. "Ms. Hubbard, I look forward to our upcoming meeting and each one after that."

I took back my hand, holding on to it too tightly. "I suggest you watch yourself, Mr. Graham. The Coopers have strict rules in place against workplace sexual harassment."

Fin lowered his voice. "During our upcoming meeting, I'll be watching to see if your nipples are as hard as they've been since you entered this office. It truly is a fantastic view." He turned and walked toward the door.

"I didn't know you had been signed," I blurted out.

He turned back. "Now you do."

"If I'd have known of the talks, I would have objected."

"While I believe you should have known—"

"Royce deals with football operations."

"You still should have been told." He shrugged. "What would you have said...to object?"

"I would have commented that you have a history that reflects a lack of commitment."

He furrowed his brow and nodded. "Commitment?"

"You played out your rookie contract in Atlanta but didn't exercise your option for an additional year. You moved to Tampa. You were only with the Buccaneers a year before you went to Green Bay. Last year you spent in LA and never stepped foot on the field. Now, you're here in Lexington. We can't count on you for the betterment of the team."

"Oh, you were talking football. I assumed—"

"Well, don't," I said.

"And here you made it seem as if you hadn't followed my career."

"I haven't," I lied. "I did my research after yesterday's game."

His cocky grin was back. "Vee, whether you believe me or not, I'm happy to see you again. You're next in line to own the Coopers. Your father or Beasley should have informed you that we were in negotiations. However, if your knowing would have resulted in me not being offered the contract, I'm glad you didn't know."

"Preston is fun to be around, charismatic, and dependable."

Fin's smile quirked. "Sounds like a collie. Does he like it when you collar him?" Before I could respond, he was gone through the doorway. He closed the door quietly behind him.

Shit.

"Ugh," I groaned as I made my way to my desk chair, collapsed, and closed my eyes. It was as if his handsome face was painted on the inside of my eyelids. Blinking rapidly, I tried to erase the image.

My thoughts raced.

To hell with Griffin Graham. Preston wasn't a dog. Collar him? What the hell did that even mean? If Fin thought I'd welcome him with open arms after the way he ran away all those years ago, he was sadly mistaken. He obviously had a commitment issue.

Royce had signed him for one year.

One year.

I picked up the phone on my desk and pushed the button for Jen. She answered right away. "Connect me with Royce Beasley."

"I'll try. I doubt he's available. Your meeting is in seven minutes."

"Seven. Shit, forget it. I'll talk to him there."

If Royce was so hellbent on keeping Fin, he could increase the salary for the one-year contract, but I'd do my best not to extend the length. Grabbing the blazer from the back of my chair, I slid my arms through the sleeves, took my tablet, and hurried toward the Carroll meeting room.

Voices could be heard as I approached the open door. Stepping inside, I assessed that almost everyone was present—everyone except for Dad, Uncle Darin, and Grant. Straightening my shoulders, I spoke. "Good afternoon, gentlemen. Royce, if you don't mind, I'd like to have a word with you."

Royce quirked a shaggy eyebrow and nodded. "We'll continue this once Reid arrives," he said to Fin and his agent, Jackson Blanch.

Together, we walked back into the hallway.

"Do you have a concern?" Royce asked.

"I do." This would be the first time I voiced my opinion regarding football operations. "I've reviewed Mr. Graham's career. I think offering increased pay for one year is acceptable. Given his age and his record of not staying for very long with a team, I feel that offering him more than a one-year contract is a mistake. If we offer him two or three years and he decides to bolt after one, it looks bad for the Coopers."

"These deals don't just materialize, Vee." He jutted his chin. "Reid can explain it to you."

I turned, seeing my father approach.

"Is there an issue?" Dad asked.

"Vee has voiced an opinion regarding Griffin Graham."

When Dad met my gaze, I repeated what I'd just told Royce and added more. "If other players see the Coopers as a revolving door, it will hurt us in the long run. Building a dynasty team is our objective."

As Royce walked back into the meeting room, Dad reached for my arm. "I just got off the phone with Brad. The accounting department has been working all morning on this. We're set for three years."

"Three?" I shook my head. "Do you know how old Fin will be in three years?"

"Like the rest of us," Dad said, "three years older than we are today." He lowered his voice. "I'm sorry you didn't bring this up earlier when we spoke. If Mr. Graham and Mr. Blanch are agreeable, the deal is set."

"The original contract was one million for one year," I said, "What are we now offering?"

Dad pressed his lips together. "This isn't the time to discuss. I came to you earlier today."

Closing my eyes, I exhaled. "Why wasn't I told ahead of time that we were making an offer to Fin— Mr. Graham?"

"This is why you're going to spend more time this year in football operations."

I was seething, my blood boiling, as we entered the meeting room, Grant and Uncle Darin on our heels.

"Royce pulled this deal out of his ass," Grant whispered.

His comment didn't help my attitude. I still didn't know the offer.

CHAPTER 9

Fin

I stood as Reid Hubbard, Vee, and Darin and Grant Marsh entered the room.

"Mr. Graham," the owner and CEO of the Coopers said, offering me his hand. "It's nice to finally meet you in person."

"Likewise," I replied, shaking his hand. While I'd seen his picture many times, as he'd said, it was our first in-person meeting. As we shook, I noticed he had Vee's eyes, or more accurately, she had his.

There were other things I wanted to say, like how after over eight months of dating, Vee never introduced me to her father. She never mentioned that he was the owner and CEO of the Lexington Coopers. Or how she didn't disclose that she was connected to a football franchise. Yes, she'd told me her name, but how was I to know that she was one of *those* Hubbards.

Back then, to me she was Vee, my Abby.

Mr. Hubbard took the seat at the head of the conference table. Behind him was a large portrait of Carroll Hubbard, the man who purchased the Coopers in 1978. I'd also done my homework.

I sat to Mr. Hubbard's right with my agent, Jackson Blanch, to my right. Royce Beasley sat across from me, Darin Marsh across from Jackson, Grant to his left, and Vee too far away. Even with the distance, I couldn't look away.

Vee's expression wasn't what I'd classify as pleased. The muscles pulled tight in her cheeks and tendons strained in her neck. Flames simmered behind her green eyes, reminding me of the fire that burned within her. That didn't mean she wasn't still beautiful. While I preferred a smile, the serious vice-president expression was sexy as hell. My thoughts went to a sultry, nerdy librarian. Yes, that was definitely the vibe I was picking up. Seeing her jacket, one matching her skirt, made me smirk. That was one way to hide the beaded nipples. However, it was too late for that; the vision of the way her blouse tented in her office was imprinted on my brain. She may have her guard up around me, but that was okay. This little meeting confirmed that I had three years to wear her down.

Forcing my attention to the head of the table, Reid Hubbard's words began to register.

"...impressed by your performance yesterday."

"Thank you, sir. Andrew Pratt" —the offensive coordinator— "wants me to start working with more of our running backs, wide receivers, and tight ends. JD and I go way back. It felt like old times."

"Tomorrow," Royce interjected, "the offensive staff is planning on Fin's working with Dennison, learning the routes and plays."

"What about Simpson?" Vee asked, her forehead furrowed in question.

Royce's head snapped her direction. "Ms. Hubbard, we can discuss that later."

My neck straightened at the condescending tone in his voice. Before I could interject, Grant leaned toward her and spoke too low to be overheard. I knew what he was saying. Royce cut Simpson to increase my contract. It had been the talk of more than a few text exchanges. Simpson was a talented quarterback and a free agent. He'd be picked up before the preseason was over.

"Do you have any questions or concerns regarding the revised contract?" Reid asked.

"Only one," Jackson replied for me. "Mr. Graham would like the option to buy out his third year, when that time comes."

Vee crossed her arms over her breasts and

hummed. Her pouty lips were pressed into a straight line.

"Ms. Hubbard," I questioned, using the name she requested, "is that stipulation upsetting to you?"

She scanned the table and lowered her arms. "I'm concerned..." She met her father's gaze before turning those gorgeous green eyes on Jackson and continuing. "Mr. Blanch, it seems that your client has an issue with commitment to one team. And the stipulation you mentioned sounds as if he's already having second thoughts about the Coopers."

"Not at all," Jackson replied. "It's a common stipulation for veteran players such as Mr. Graham. Barring injury, my client is willing to stay the full three years. However, in the case of injury, this creates a possible exit route for both Fin and the Coopers."

Vee nodded.

The discussion continued, Royce Beasley and Jackson doing most of the talking.

The original contract was one million dollars for one year. This revised contract was four million dollars per year for three years. There was also a signing bonus of three million dollars and the promise of a performance bonus contingent upon the amount of playing time I received. The increased salary was the reason for Simpson's dismissal.

No one disputed the first-string quarterback Troy Dennison's ability. This early in his career, there were warranted comparisons to the likes of Tom Brady or Peyton Manning. With a first-string quarterback like Dennison, Jackson didn't want me in third place.

When it seemed like both sides were satisfied, Mr. Hubbard spoke. "Welcome officially to the Coopers, Mr. Graham."

"Please call me Fin, Mr. Hubbard."

"Fin, we can't wait to see what you can do for us and what we can do for you."

I leaned back. "I'm originally from Kentucky, Bowling Green to be exact." My gaze momentarily went to Vee. This wasn't news to her. She'd visited my parents in Bowling Green. "I'm looking forward to returning to the Bluegrass state and being closer to my family."

A knock came from the door. It opened and Coach Tilson and Andrew Pratt stepped inside.

"I'm sorry we couldn't be here sooner," Coach Tilson said, his gaze meeting Reid's. "Do we have our new number two?"

"We do," Reid announced.

Pratt turned to me. "Fin, stop by my office after your position meeting. Noah and I want to talk to you about specifics. We only have one more preseason game before the real season starts. Now that you're officially playing behind Dennison, we need you up-to-date on every play."

Noah Garcia was the quarterback coach. "I'll be there, Coach."

Pratt leaned between Grant and Vee and whispered something. While Grant appeared unaffected, Vee's complexion paled. He patted her shoulder.

"I'll be there," she said.

What in the fuck was going on behind the scenes with this organization?

CHAPTER 10

Vee

Rubbing my temples, I couldn't ignore the thumping in my head. If asked, I'd say that I was certain my head was about to explode. Opening my water bottle, I took a long swig. The playbook in front of me was akin to a foreign language. Dad was right. Football operations was the part of our franchise I needed to understand at a higher level.

Talk to me about the ROI on television ads that showcased our mascot versus those that showed fans in the stadium or players on the field. Ask me how long it took to change the field from artificial turf to a trade show with over three hundred exhibitions. How many workers per hour to accomplish an end game? I could rattle off the numbers without so much as a second thought. Our ticket sales were a case study in football sales. I spent an untold amount of time comparing prices throughout the NFL.

Even with that knowledge base, the words before me were maddening.

I knew the positions both offense and defense, eleven players on the field per side. I'd watched enough games to understand what each position was supposed to accomplish, and which defensive player was responsible for what offensive player. However, after the meeting with Fin, I did as Andrew Pratt asked and made my way into the unknown, the offices in football operation.

Our players were in various places around Maker's Mark Football Center. The athletic trainers were already assessing yesterday's injuries. The coaches met first with the entire team to discuss what they learned from films. Then the players had position meetings, talking with their specific coaches for each position. Fin and Troy Dennison would be in the quarterback discussion.

I shook my head, thinking about Simpson. He'd been with the Coopers for three years. Correction, this would have been his third year. Now, he was gone, Griffin Graham in his place.

When I was at the University of Kentucky, I stood

on the sidelines during practices and games. I listened to the play calling but never tried to understand it. The basics were ingrained. Making sense of the unknown was the assignment Coach Pratt gave me—my homework, it could be said.

It was nearly five o'clock, and I'd been studying the offensive playbook I was given and had half of a notebook filled with notes. In two days—Wednesday morning—Pratt wanted me on the sidelines for the first practice session in preparation for next Sunday's game. That gave me roughly thirty-six hours to make heads or tails out of this foreign language.

The play before me read: *Green Rt Slot 'Z' Rt. 96 Boss, On two, On two, ready break.*

Thirty-six hours wouldn't be enough.

I reached for my cell phone and suddenly realized I'd turned off the volume for the first meeting of the day and hadn't checked it since. There were two missed calls and three text messages from Preston.

"Collie," I said under my breath. My thoughts tried to come up with a more positive image, but in reality, collies were cute, energetic, lovable, and loyal. That wasn't a negative assessment. Of course, they could be exhausting and maybe annoying.

The term was eerily close to accurate.

The first two text messages were nothing of importance. It was the third that seemed more urgent.

· · ·

"VEE, I'VE BEEN TRYING ALL DAY TO REACH YOU. CALL ME."

THE TEXT WAS SENT over an hour ago.

I hit the call icon. Preston answered on the second ring.

"Fuck, Vee," his voice roared. "Now you're not returning my calls."

"Whoa," I said in my most assertive tone. "I am returning your call. I'm at work. Mondays are filled with meetings. You know that. What was so urgent that you needed to talk to me?"

He exhaled. "Meadow Farms' top sire broke his leg. A freak accident. He stumbled into a hole in the pasture."

I heard Preston's concern as my nose scrunched. "I don't know that much about horses, but that's bad, right?"

"Yeah, it's bad." He huffed. "It would be nice if you tried to understand my family business. No, it's always about yours." He took a breath. "Think of it like Dennison breaking his leg."

"I mean," I said, "We wouldn't shoot Dennison if he broke his leg. What's going to happen to the stallion?"

"The veterinary team is assessing him, but there's a good chance he'll be put down."

"It's not like he's racing anymore. He's just...screwing. That doesn't take four healthy legs."

"You've got a lot to learn about stallions and thoroughbreds."

Yeah, apparently, I had a lot to learn about a wide range of subjects. Before I could respond, he went on.

"I wanted to talk to you because I'm on my way to Meadow Farms. I'll be gone a couple days."

"Okay."

"Damn it, Vee." His voice was louder than necessary. "Are you happy I'm going to be gone?"

"No," I answered too quickly to give the question the time it deserved. "It's not about you, all right?"

"Of course not. It's always about you."

"Preston..."

"It sure as hell seems that way. You've been cold as ice since Saturday night."

"My father has decided I need to be better prepared for ownership. He wants me to spend more time in football operations. The offensive coordinator gave me homework. I'm supposed to learn a hundred or more play calls by Wednesday. So, no, Preston, I'm not happy you're going out of town. I sure as hell won't rejoice in some super stud horse being injured or euthanized. I'm simply busy."

Preston's tone softened. "Why exactly does Reid want you to spend more time in football operations?

You're vice president of stadium operations and marketing."

Placing my elbow on my desk, I held my head and sighed. "Dad's right. He and Drew Pratt are pushing this. I should understand the football side of the Coopers."

"So you'll be around that new Griffin guy more."

It wasn't a question, but I answered, "Seriously, Preston. I'll be around the entire team. Besides, I think Dad is right; I should know more. I hope Dad's around for a long time, but when the time comes for me to make multimillion-dollar decisions, I should understand what they entail. I think Royce is behind the playbook memorization. Drew mentioned his name. Royce is a sexist asshole who wants me to give up or fail."

"My Vee isn't a failure or a quitter."

"Thanks," I said.

"That bastard Beasley should retire."

The first smile of our conversation curled my lips. "That would be great news." I lifted my head. "Drive safely. I hope the stallion can be healed."

"My dad's upset, but the truth is we've got a lot of frozen sperm. Maximus can go on to sire great stallions for years." There was a pause. "Vee, are we good?"

Fun to be around.

Charismatic.

Dependable.

A collie.

"I want us to be," I answered honestly. "Leigh thinks I have commitment issues." As the words came out of my mouth, I remembered telling Fin he had the same issue.

"Leigh's wrong. I'll call you when I know when I'm returning. Let's go out, a date, just the two of us. After all your memorization, you can rattle off play calls, and I can try to figure them out."

A laugh bubbled from my lips. "Yes, to a date. No, to play calls."

"Sounds good. Vee, I love you."

No, it wasn't the first time he'd said it. That didn't make it sound less confining, like my clothes were shrinking around me. "Yeah. Stay safe and call me." I hit the disconnect button and laid the phone on my desk as my office door opened.

Jen peeked around the door jamb. "It's after five. I'm headed out. Do you need anything before I go?"

"Do you know how to decipher offensive play calls?"

She pursed her lips. "Sorry, no."

"It's okay." I stood, pushing back my chair. "I think I'll head home too. I'd rather go through these plays in pajama pants and without a bra."

Jen laughed. "I'll see you tomorrow."

With my tablet, Pratt's playbook, and other essentials in my leather tote, I made my way out of the football center, adding one more person to the mad exodus. My mind was on the play calls, trying to come up with a system to remember them when I looked up. The large black truck parked beside my car belonged to our newest signed quarterback. I wouldn't have known if not for the handsome man standing at the driver's door.

CHAPTER 11

Vee

It was a split-second decision. Would I acknowledge Fin's presence, or just pretend not to see him?

"Ms. Hubbard," he said, spotting me coming closer. "Are you stalking me? I hear that the Coopers has strict sexual harassment rules. I'd hate to have to report you to HR." His smile was too wide to be serious.

"Walking to my car." I stopped near my tailgate. My white Mercedes-Benz AMG GT 63 was dwarfed beside his monstrous truck. I lifted a brow. "Overcompensating, are we?"

Fin laughed. "Not even in the slightest."

In the Kentucky heat, he leaned against the side panel and crossed his ankles. Although his blue stare was covered by sunglasses, I felt their focus singeing my skin. The button-down shirt was wrinkle free, except the sleeves were now rolled, showcasing his tanned forearms. Fin looked as put together as he had earlier in my office. Me on the other hand...I wished I'd worn my jacket. I couldn't exactly blame hard nipples on the eighty-three-degree day.

"I like a vehicle that can actually carry things, people, cargo, whatever I might need."

"I suppose it comes in handy for someone who moves around as much as you do. No need to hire a moving company."

Fin tipped his chin toward my car. "With that tiny back seat, how do you even grocery shop?"

My head tilted to the side. "I avoid buying in bulk."

Fin nodded. "It really is good to see you again."

I nodded. "You look good."

"You too. You always have."

Inhaling, I shook my head. "We can try not to make things awkward. No one knows our history except my cousins Lip and Leigh."

"I was thinking about that when I met Mr. Hubbard. I was never given an opportunity to meet him years ago."

"You don't understand what it was like, being

around the football team at Kentucky. If anyone had known I was part of the Lexington Coopers' Hubbards, I would have been treated differently. Only the coach knew."

"I thought you and I were closer than you and the rest of the team."

Pressing my lips together, I shook my head. "Sorry, Fin. I don't have time for this, now or ever," I added. "I need to go." I lifted my tote. "Drew Pratt gave me homework."

"Aren't you his boss?"

"No. That would be Royce, Dad, Uncle Darin, and I suppose, Grant. Like I said earlier, I concentrate on the business side of the franchise."

He stepped away from the truck as his forehead furrowed. "Then why is Pratt giving you homework?"

"It's my father's idea. He wants me to have an understanding of both sides of the team."

Fin cocked his eyebrows. "Does that mean I might be seeing more of you?"

"If I pass Royce's test. I think he doesn't believe I will."

"What's his test?"

I pulled the playbook out of my tote bag. "Learn some one hundred play calls by Wednesday morning practice."

"I have the same homework. Let me know if you

want a study buddy. I still owe you for helping me with economics."

"Managerial economics," I specified, "and you were the one who worked your ass off."

"I'm still willing to return the favor." Fin came closer. "Let me see your phone."

I narrowed my gaze. "Why?"

"I want to add my number. That way if you need help, you can call."

"Fin." I sighed. "I'm not going to call you."

He lifted his hand palm up.

Next thing I knew, I pulled my phone from the tote bag and laid it in his large hand.

"Lock screen code?"

"Some things a woman doesn't share," I said with a grin, retrieving my phone. After entering the lock screen code, I handed it back.

Fin took the phone and began swiping the screen. "There." His firm lips twitched into a grin.

Reaching to take my phone back, our hands grazed each other's. Electricity skirted over my flesh. Pulling my hand back, I said, "I need to go."

"Yeah, see you around, Ms. Hubbard."

"Vee."

His grin blossomed. "I'll take that as a positive move forward."

I didn't respond as we both got into our respective vehicles.

For a moment, I stared at the dashboard as I brought the car to life. The screen to my right let me know my cell phone was connected. I had one unread text.

While I didn't recognize the number, I hit the screen, asking my car to read it to me.

"Message from ###-###-####. Name the time and place."

I furrowed my brow. What kind of text was that?

Lifting my phone, I read the text message. It wasn't so much a message, but a response.

From me:

"FIN, GREAT TO SEE YOU. LET'S CATCH UP."

FROM THE UNKNOWN NUMBER:

"NAME THE TIME AND THE PLACE."

HE DIDN'T ONLY GIVE me his number, but he shared my number with him.

I looked up. Fin's truck was gone from the parking space. Tossing my phone back into my tote, I laid my head back on the soft seat and tried to reason with my traitorous memories. It seemed to me that I should be recalling the way he ghosted me. I should be remembering the nights I waited for him to call or text.

Why, instead, was I recalling more favorable things about Fin Graham?

---

*NEARLY FOURTEEN YEARS **ago***

"OH, Fin is going to freak the fuck out when he sees you," Emma said, standing behind me as we both gazed into the full-length mirror. She ran her hands over my long curls, the ones she'd worked so hard to create. Crystal combs held the sides up, leaving small spirals dangling near my cheeks. Diamond studs matching the diamond solitaire necklace glistened. Both were my high school graduation gifts from Dad and Daphne.

I smoothed the skirt of my dress. "You don't think it's too short, do you?" The red satin dress came to my midthighs. The neckline required a strapless bra, and my heels were dangerously high for a Delta Tau Delta fraternity New Year's Eve dance.

"Are you kidding?" my friend asked. "You're gorgeous. Fin will want to screw you as soon as he sees you."

I turned, meeting Emma's gaze. "We still haven't... gone all the way."

She opened her eyes wide. "It's been what, like a year?"

"Almost six months," I corrected. "We've done a lot, well, like everything else. This dance feels like prom. Like tonight will be the night." My cheeks warmed. "Fin reserved a hotel room for after the dance."

"Thank God I won't have to hear the two of you through these thin walls." Emma reached for my shoulders and turned me toward her. "Just because he reserved a room doesn't mean you have to go all the way. You don't owe it to him."

I wiggled my shoulders, looking directly into her eyes. "I want to. I want it to be Fin. I've never felt like this before." I tried to tame my smile. "He doesn't know who my dad is or what he does. Fin loves football, but it seems like he might love me too. For me." I sighed. "Does that make sense? The guys in high school all knew who I was. It would have been a notch in their belt to take Reid Hubbard's only daughter's virginity. Fin...he's different."

Emma's cheeks rose as her smile softened. "Fuck all the guys back at your high school. You're Vee Hubbard. You don't have to be Reid Hubbard's daughter."

My gaze again went to the mirror. I scanned my chestnut hair down my red dress, to my legs, and the high heels. "I'm twenty years old. I think I'm ready."

Emma smirked. "Make Fin work for it. Don't be so willing."

I giggled at memories. "He's been working for it. I promise."

"Oh, details."

I shook my head, the small curls swaying near my face. "Not yet." God knew that Emma had shared too many details with me. "I need to savor them a little longer."

"Oral?" she asked.

"I'm not saying." Despite my stand, warmth filled my cheeks at the memory of Fin going down on me. He'd done that more than a few times before I braved going down on him. His size was a problem. In books it sounded good, but in reality, I had to use my hands to surround him. Even without experience, I had the sensation of being the one girl who could make the great Fin Graham come apart.

While the football season was over, University of Kentucky had made it to a bowl game for the first time in five years. We played Georgia Tech in the Tax Slayer Bowl—the bowl names nowadays were crazy. We lost 18–33, but the talking heads on college football had nothing but praise for Griffin Graham, saying he was the key to our successful season.

"Vee, the look in your eyes tells me all I need to know." She took on her mother tone. "Do you have protection? I have some condoms in my room. I could let you have a few."

"A few? Do we need more than one?"

Emma laughed. "That depends on a few different things, but from my experience, it's better to be prepared."

"If you let me have two, I'll buy you more."

She shook her head. "Consider them my gift." Her smile grew. "Fin's a lucky guy."

"I hope he agrees." I also hoped he would choose to stay at UK. His dad had been hounding him about the transfer portal which would be open for the next two weeks.

The doorbell to our apartment rang, reverberating through the rooms.

Emma's smile grew even larger. "We're about to find out. Let me go let him in. Then you can make a grand entrance."

I nodded.

Fin's deep voice came from the other room as I bravely opened my bedroom door and stepped into the small hallway. He was near the front door when Emma stepped aside. Fin's blue stare scanned me from my toes to my hair, taking in every inch of me as if he was seeing what was hidden.

From my direction, I scanned him too, also knowing what was beneath his dark gray suit. His red tie matched my dress. While I hadn't been sure if it was possible for Fin to look sexier than he did in his uniform, tonight I knew it was. And yet, I was waiting to hear his reaction.

"Fuck, Abby, you're stunning."

My heart melted to goo.

"Looking good yourself."

CHAPTER 12

Vee

Present time

Tuesday morning flew by as I met with other members of my marketing team. There were even moments when I forgot that the new hire had tilted the axis of my world. The fact that most of the players were away from Maker's Mark Football Center helped. The few who were present were here to work on injuries. Thankfully, the players who ended up on the injury report after Sunday's game weren't seriously injured. Our backup running back had an ankle sprain, and two of our defensive players were being treated for shoulder injuries.

With my afternoon clear of meetings and obligations, I told Jen to hold all calls, and I barricaded myself in my office. Drew's playbook was open on my small conference table, and I set up a makeshift offense consisting of eleven red checkers. I'd taped initials to each piece, indicating their position. It may sound silly, but I was a visual learner. Once I deciphered a call, I ran it on my table, moving my offense as they were supposed to go. The receivers ran routes and the running backs ran gaps. Of course, my crude setup didn't have a defense ready to tackle or stop them. I was only focused on the offense.

The more I studied, the more the words made sense. I knew from collaborating with Coach Everington that each team had their own language. A quarterback couldn't shout play calls in ways the defense would be able to understand. It wasn't like Troy or Fin could yell, "Okay guys, we're going to run a fake handoff to Dijon, then I'm going to step back, read my open receivers left to right. Patel, you run an out route, JD, a corner route, Lewis a comeback, Bennett a dig, and Morgan a post."

If they did that, the defense would have the information they needed for man-to-man coverage, and the play would get shut down. Instead, each team has substitute words, letters, or numbers. While the playbook was overwhelming at first, sometime last night in my quiet apartment, I caught on to the redundancy and made a list of terms and their meanings.

It really was like a foreign language.

I was working out a long play.

Explode gun rubber right flip zebra stat left wide drag X hook F-trail can 52 sprint jaw easy on two on two. Ready break.

I was moving my pieces around when my desk phone rang.

The ring set off my nerves and pulled me from the zone I'd been in. "I told her no calls," I mumbled as I made my way over to the phone. "Jen, I said I didn't want to be disturbed."

"I'm sorry, Vee. Mr. Grant Marsh is here. He's rather insistent that he speak to you."

My cousin.

Exhaling, I complied. "Let him in."

"Right away."

A few seconds later, my door opened, Grant entered and closed the door. When he turned, his expression was difficult to read.

"Aren't you on the wrong side of the building?" I asked. As vice president of communications, Grant's offices were more connected to the football operations section of Maker's Mark Football Center.

"I came to check on you."

Walking around to the front of my desk, I leaned

against it and crossed my arms over my breasts. "A wellness check on your favorite cousin."

"You're my only cousin." He lifted his hand. "I mean, if you're ready for Drew tomorrow, I'll leave you alone. I just didn't want to see my only cousin faltering in front of the team."

Dropping my arms, I exhaled. "Thank you for your vote of confidence."

"Vee, you're great at what you do. I get why Uncle Reid wants you to get your feet wet on the football operations side. It's that failing won't instill confidence in the Coopers' staff or players. I've been thinking about it. I've been working with the Coopers nearly twice as long as you have. My job is communications. I don't want a weak link to threaten our brand."

My lips pursed as I tilted my head. "Why do I have the feeling I'm about to be mansplained?"

"It's not mansplaining, other than I'm a man and I want to explain."

Totally different.

"Great. Explain," I said.

"You excel here, in stadium operations and marketing. I've spent the last eighteen years in communications and broadcasting. Uncle Reid has had most of his attention on business operations. Lip is the chief brand officer. We all have our roles. Together we can convince Uncle Reid that your presence in the football side is a waste of time."

"A waste of time? Your mother has announced she wants to retire. That's why Dad wants me to step up my presence in football operations."

"Uncle Reid and Dad aren't going anywhere anytime soon. When that time comes, we divide up the oversight as they've done."

I narrowed my eyes. "Just so I'm clear on what you're suggesting, you think that once the team is in my control, I should simply trust someone else with the running of football operations without actually knowing the ins and outs."

"Vee, you won't be the sole owner. Dad told Lip and me that the team will be broken into three parts."

My neck straightened. "I believe you're mistaken. Besides, why would Dad include you and Lip and not Leigh?"

"You'll need to ask him. I'll tell Drew and Royce that you won't be able to make practice tomorrow."

"No, Grant, you won't. I will be there, doing what Dad asked of me."

"Vee, I'm offering this for your own good. The Coopers rely primarily on the Erhardt-Perkins call system. It's complicated."

"If you can figure it out, I doubt I'll have a problem." My lips curled. "Grant, I'm so grateful for your visit. I'll be ready tomorrow, don't worry."

"It's your funeral. The respect you've earned over the years will disintegrate."

"Your confidence is flattering."

"I saw your expression yesterday when Drew told you to be at tomorrow's practice. You've never been good at poker. You went pale."

I began walking toward the door. "Thanks for stopping by. It's kind of you to be concerned." I opened the door. "I'll see you tomorrow."

As I began to close the door, I heard multiple deep male voices.

Shit.

A quick peek around the corner and I saw Grant and Fin in Jen's office. While my cousin was wearing his usual business casual, Fin was wearing very casual attire—a t-shirt and gym shorts. If I was in the mood to smile, I would at the sight of Fin towering over Grant.

I inhaled. "Jen, please ask everyone to leave."

She looked at me with a pained expression. "I have."

"Excuse me," I said louder. When Fin and Grant turned my way, I widened my eyes. "Please continue your conversation elsewhere." When neither replied, I asked, "Fin, why are you at Maker's Mark today? Did you need to see the trainers?"

Is he injured?

Do I care beyond the business aspect?

His name wasn't on the IR.

"I came to speak to you."

"Came all the way here to speak to me?"

"I did."

Shit. It would be rude to turn him away. I spoke to Grant. "We're done. I'll see you tomorrow."

"How's Preston, Vee?" my cousin asked.

"He's great. I'll pass on your concern for him."

As Grant walked through Jen's open doorway, I waved Fin into my office. Once inside, I closed the door.

Turning, I met Fin's blue gaze. There was more facial hair on his cheeks than there was yesterday. His hair was damp and a clean scent permeated the air. "Please make this fast. I'm in crunch mode and would like to stay focused."

"I came to Maker's today to work out. As you know, you have a great fitness center."

"And now you're here...in my office, why?" I asked.

"I've been thinking about the test you have tomorrow. I came by to see how you're doing with your studying."

I crossed my arms over my breasts. "If you're here to tell me I can't possibly succeed, you're too late. Grant already beat you to it."

Fin took a step closer, searching my face. "He's wrong. I didn't come to say that. I know how fucking intelligent you are. I thought since I've had the playbook a week longer, if you had questions.... You can always call Beasley or there's your cousin."

"I'd venture to say that they both expect my failure."

Fin pressed his lips together and shook his head. "Not me." He pivoted to the door and back. "I'll go. You didn't call. I wanted you to know I'm still available for a study session."

CHAPTER 13

Vee

"Do you want to see what I've done?" I wasn't sure why I blurted out the question. Probably because I was upset by Grant's lack of confidence in me, not that it was out of character. Maybe I wanted to hear Fin tell me he had faith in my ability. Whatever the reason, the question was out, and instead of leaving, Fin stared at me with a grin. "Come over here." I led him to the conference table.

"You're playing a game of checkers with half the pieces and no board?"

"It's the offense." I picked up the one with QB taped

to the top. "That's you." I shrugged. "Or Troy. I'm using positions not names."

Fin picked up my notebook. The one with the translations for each word. "Where did you get this?"

"I made it last night. The playbook has schematics. I was able to figure out what each word, number, or letter meant." I shrugged. "Most of them. I have a few blanks."

"Vee, this is amazing. I know veteran players who don't pick up on the cadence this quick."

While I hated admitting it, even to myself, I appreciated Fin's approval. "I'll need to refer to my notes, but I think I have a handle on practice tomorrow. I've told myself to approach the play calls like a foreign language."

The praise in his gaze warmed me from the inside.

"Let me quiz you."

I snagged my lower lip between my teeth. "I'm not ready to go without my notes."

"Use your notes." He pulled out one of the chairs across the table and picked up the playbook Drew had given me. "Let me look..."

I moved my players into formation.

Fin scrutinized the placement. "What if we're not in *I* formation?"

Lifting my face, I met his stare with a furrowed brow. "I hadn't thought of that."

"*I* formation is the most common. But let me show

you a few others." He reached for two backs and moved them side by side. "This is the split back."

"Why would you want a split back formation?"

"It puts the running back and fullback closer to the quarterback. After the snap, the quarterback can easily pass or fake a pass. They both pretend they have the ball and divide the defense."

A smile curled my lips. "And you can step back and throw down the field."

"That's the plan. Line up in split back formation, and I'll call a play."

I moved the checkers into the formation he'd just shown me.

"Ready?"

"Ready," I replied.

"Double right 200 jet dragon."

I looked down at my notes and back up at Fin.

"Do you—?"

"Shh." I left the checkers in split formation but widened the distance between the two backs. The offensive line moved forward, as if ready to block. The running backs both ran a *slant* while the outside receivers ran an *in* route. The tight end ran a *post*. "If he's open" —I point to the tight end— "he gets the pass. If not, it goes to one of the backs or receivers. That's your decision."

"What if they're all blocked?" he asked.

"It's hard to say without calculating for the defense."

Fin reached for the QB checker. "My job is to go through my reads." He touched each of the eligible receivers. "I move from one to the next, seeing if they're on the right route and what the defense is doing. If all my targets are covered, I run the ball or ground it. Anything but a sack."

"Can we do this again?" I asked.

"Sure. Let me show you some other formations."

Fin explained the twins, ace, trips, empty, and quads formations. With each setup, he explained why it would be called and what likely calls would be used. Each time he read me a call, I checked my notes and moved the checkers.

"We're pretending this is no-huddle offense," Fin said. "Huddle calls tend to be longer. You want to try?"

"Yes," I replied eagerly.

Time got away from us as we moved the checkers over the table.

"Oh my goodness," I said, looking at my watch. "It's after seven. Jen didn't tell me she was leaving."

"I believe you told her you didn't want to be disturbed, or that's what she told me when I arrived."

My smile lifted my cheeks. "I'm glad you didn't listen. This" —I motioned to the checkers— "was very helpful."

"You're the one who came up with the idea."

"I don't like the diagrams. I want something more concrete."

Fin pushed back his chair and stood. "You're going to do great tomorrow."

"Thank you for checking on me." I'd forgotten about his attire. My gaze went to his muscular legs, up to his waist, and the way the Coopers t-shirt tapered out to his wide shoulders. "We should call it a night."

"I'd ask you to dinner, but I'm not exactly dressed for dining. Unless it's McDonald's."

"Don't make me tell Drew. McDonald's is not on the Coopers-approved list for proper nutrition."

Fin laughed. "I can't remember the last time I ate fast food."

"Keep it that way."

He touched his forehead with two fingers in a salute. "Yes, boss. Maybe a raincheck on the dinner thing?"

A sigh came from my lips. "I probably shouldn't, unless you want to bring a date. We can double date."

"No offense, but I don't want to have dinner with Preston Clark."

"Do you know him?"

"Not him. I know his family. Back when I lived in Bowling Green. They were..." He inhaled. "Their reputation wasn't favorable with local people, especially those who worked in the horse industry."

"Meadow Farms has been in the Clark family for

generations." I wasn't sure why I felt the need to defend Preston's family. "They've always been nice to me."

"Sure, because you have money."

"You're saying that you don't actually know Preston?"

"I do not," he conceded. "I suppose I shouldn't make blanket judgments."

I nodded with a grin. "Thank you for reconsidering. Let me know when you want to double date."

"That answer," he said with a sexy quirk to his grin, "won't change. I can walk you to your car."

Turning toward the windows, I saw the summer evening sky. "It's not dark. I'll be fine. Thanks."

"Do you have more work to do?"

"No."

"Then grab your things," he said. "You can't trust the football types around here."

"I happen to spend all my time here. I'm safe."

"Vee, let me get to spend a few more minutes with you."

"You're bossy."

"I can be," he said, "especially when I know what I want."

Ignoring that comment or the way it made my insides twist, I took the playbook and walked to my desk. I collected my tablet and put everything into my tote. "I'm ready."

CHAPTER 14

Fin

Wednesday morning, the locker room buzzed with the usual first day of the week subjects. Players compared their day off. They talked about their wives, girlfriends, and kids. A few people were still lamenting last Sunday's loss. That was the minority. Monday was for rehashing. After that you moved on. Tuesday was rest and on Wednesday the team began anew. The same was true after a win. A team that was still celebrating on the following Wednesday would lose on the next Sunday. Each week was a race. Seventeen games to win, before the real marathon began—the race to the Super Bowl.

Next Sunday's opponent was the Detroit Lions.

Last season they had a fifteen and two record. Then unexpectedly they were eliminated in the first game of the postseason. It wasn't a secret that the Lions were out to make up for the playoff loss. While I was in LA last season, being on the West Coast didn't mean I hadn't kept up with all the teams.

I'd been monitoring the Coopers for most of my career. While I respected the organization, it was the woman I'd spent yesterday afternoon with who was my main pull. I meant what I told her. Life was moving forward and I had my sights on Maeve Hubbard for that next quarter.

I definitely didn't feel that way when I transferred to Tennessee. Vee never mentioned her family's connection to the Coopers. She didn't keep her name a secret. She talked about her father, stepmother, and cousin Leigh. Rarely, she mentioned her mother.

In hindsight, maybe I could have put the clues together—I hadn't.

It wasn't until I transferred to Tennessee that I learned she was part of the Coopers' Hubbards. Learning the part of her that she'd kept secret felt like a betrayal—a real punch in the gut. Vee knew my aspirations and instead of inviting me to meet Reid Hubbard, she kept him a secret. At twenty-two years old, I was pissed.

Before I transferred away from the University of Kentucky, I'd told her we could still talk and get together. It wasn't goodbye but instead, see you later. I'd meant that when I said it. But learning what she'd kept from me was too much. Throughout our entire relationship we'd shared a lot, and still, that lack of honesty was difficult to take.

I didn't follow through.

Now that I was here with the Coopers, I wanted a second chance. The other night in the parking lot, she said only the coach at UK knew her father owned the Coopers. She said people would have treated her differently. She was probably right. I hadn't been able to look at it that way all those years ago.

The way she looked yesterday in her office, her smiles and enthusiasm, reminded me of the Vee I once knew.

"Fin, catch."

I spun around just in time to catch a soft pass from Troy Dennison.

"Whoa."

"I'm better at throwing than catching," I said, tossing the ball back. Dennison caught it with a smile. He was ready with his full pads and practice jersey on. I was still lacing up my pants.

"Coach Garcia wants us to run some reps together after the team practice. I'm available if you are."

"Sounds like a plan."

"Word around the team is you came in to work out yesterday."

"Is that a problem?" I asked.

"No, man. Just surprising. Most take the day to chill."

I nodded. "I just moved into an apartment north of the facility. It's okay, but Maker's has better equipment than my clubhouse."

"Next Tuesday, I'll meet you over here," Dennison said before lowering his voice. "I got to tell you, it's weird being first string to you. I watched you play for Green Bay growing up. I wanted to be you."

Pulling my practice jersey over my pads, I returned his smile. Dennison was a good-looking kid, about an inch taller than me, equally as muscular with a killer smile, and short dreads. "It's not weird, and thanks. It's the way it goes with the game. I'm lucky to still be playing. Players I started with who played more demanding positions have made the right move and retired."

"You're not retiring, Fin. I'm planning on learning a lot from you." He slapped my shoulder pad. "I'll see you out there."

Starting with a new team wasn't the easiest; however, I'd done it many times. I was accustomed to being the new guy. It was more difficult to enter a new team during the season. There was camaraderie that grew between teammates with each game, win, and loss.

Simpson had that familiarity with the other players on the Coopers. Now, he'd been let go because of me.

At least it didn't sound like Dennison was holding a grudge.

Preseason was a better time to join a team. It was similar to starting a new school at the beginning of the year, versus halfway through. Instead of being in high school, I was a thirty-six-year-old man, surrounded by talented-as-hell high schoolers. They weren't that young, but sometimes it sure as hell felt that way.

Troy Dennison was only twenty-three years old. He grew up watching me play. I was thirteen years old when he was born and had already been playing football for three years. The way of the game. Out with the old and in with the new.

Our coaches spent a good chunk of yesterday watching films of the Lions and putting together a game plan. The calls they'd be making this week were ones they felt were best against the Lions' defense. And the defensive coaches will do the same to stop the Lions' offense.

Carrying my helmet, I walked outside.

I squinted my eyes at the bright sunlight.

Damn, it was going to get hot.

There were players about to practice who wouldn't be on the team come regular season. The Coopers started preseason with a ninety-player roster. That number had to be down to fifty-three and only forty-eight on the active roster by a week from Sunday. Scanning the faces, I wondered who was on the chopping block.

With my new contract, I was certain of one thing.

It wasn't me.

My smile returned as I saw Vee on the sidelines talking with Drew Pratt, our offensive coordinator, and Grant Marsh, Vee's cousin. Her long hair was pulled back in a ponytail. Unlike the business attire she had on yesterday, her sexy legs were covered by black leggings. The Coopers t-shirt hung to her mid thighs. Instead of heels, she was wearing tennis shoes. I had a flashback of her at Kentucky running onto the field with a water bottle. I should have realized there was more to her love of the game.

It looked like Vee was showing Drew her notes, and he was nodding. "You go, girl," I said under my breath. "You've got this."

That was what my text message said that I sent to Vee this morning.

She sent me back a thumbs-up emoji.

"All right, gentlemen," Coach Tilson called into a bullhorn. "Let's get ready to take down the Lions."

Everyone lifted their helmets in the air with a roar.

CHAPTER 15

Vee

Drew's lips moved but I didn't hear what he said.

I plucked the earpiece from my ear. "I'm sorry, what?"

Drew smiled. "How are you doing?"

The end of the morning practice had just been announced. "My head's swimming, but I'm not drowning."

Approval shone in his smiling expression. "You're doing well."

Andrew Pratt was in his mid-fifties. He played college football at Notre Dame. Instead of playing in the NFL, Drew went straight into coaching, first at a high school in Indiana. Then he moved up to coaching in Division III college. About ten years ago, he made the move to the NFL. He coached offense at New Orleans and Buffalo before coming to the Coopers as a quarterback coach three years ago. Dad felt he had more talent and moved him up to offensive coordinator last year. The difference between Drew and Royce Beasley was that I'd been a part of the Coopers when Drew arrived. He knew me as part of the administration despite my age and gender.

"The plays are called fast," I said. "My notes are well and good, but I need to keep working so I don't need to refer to them as often."

"You'll be surprised. The language will become second nature. Soon, you'll be hearing play calls in your dreams."

"I hope not."

Drew laughed.

"It's exciting," I said, honestly invigorated, "being this close to the action."

He patted my shoulder. "I'm glad you're here, Vee."

"Thanks, Drew. You can pass that on to Royce and Grant. Neither one of them thought I could do it."

"They're wrong."

"Who's wrong?"

Drew and I turned as my cousin approached. Before I could tell him that *he* was wrong, he spoke.

"Tell me the truth, Drew," Grant said. "Is Vee cut out for the sideline?"

"I'd welcome her any day. She has a real knack for catching on. I'm sure stadium operations and marketing doesn't want to lose you," Drew said to me, "but you're welcome here as much as your schedule allows."

Grant remained quiet as Drew walked away. Once our offensive coordinator was gone, my cousin puckered his lips and blew. "Damn, you kissed some ass."

"I think the word you're looking for is *kicked*."

"Offense is only half of the game. I was at the defense practice this morning. I'll talk to Darius Brown. He's our—"

"Stop being so fucking condescending," I interrupted. "I know who Darius is. He's our defensive coordinator. I could list the position coaches for you too, but you're not worth the effort." When Grant didn't reply, I went on, "I'm going to stay with the offense for now. I don't half-ass things. Once I'm more comfortable with the offense, I'll learn about the defense."

Grant lifted his hands, palms toward me. "Fine. I gave you an out yesterday."

"I don't need you to save me."

He quirked his eyebrows. "Speaking of yesterday, I went back to your office around five. Jen told me that you were still in your office with Griffin Graham. Did you mention that long one-on-one meeting when you went home to Preston?"

"Preston and I don't live together, not that my living arrangements are any of your damn business."

"You spoke, right? I'm talking about the man you're supposed to be seeing."

The small hairs on the back of my neck stood to attention. "Preston and I had a short conversation as I was driving home. He's busy in Bowling Green with Meadow Farms business."

"Convenient. I get it; you didn't mention the Fin meeting. What were you two talking about for hours?"

Taking off my sunglasses, I stared at Grant. "Why did you come back to my office?"

"Giving you another chance to get out of this."

I shook my head. "I'm getting some lunch and checking my emails."

"This afternoon is position practice."

"Drew gave me a schedule. Don't you have something you need to do, maybe with communications?"

"You're right. I do."

"I'm going," I said as I walked away.

I placed my sunglasses on the top of my head as I entered the building. The air conditioning cooled my skin, covering my arms with goose bumps. There was an hour and a half before the next practice session. My growling stomach wanted me to go to lunch before emails.

The tables in the cafeteria were filling fast. Some of the players appeared to have showered, while others looked sweatier rather than water wet. They were all out of their pads and practice uniforms and wearing t-shirts, nylon shorts, and basketball shoes. Their attire made me grin, reminding me of what Fin wore yesterday.

"Welcome, Miss Maeve," Janice, one of the Coopers' top nutritionists, said, meeting me near the entrance. "I heard you were out with the practice this morning."

"Rumors travel fast."

"I overheard some talk. Sounds like you impressed Mr. Pratt."

I lifted my cheeks in a smile. "I'm glad you didn't overhear that I was a royal screwup or in the way."

Janice laughed. "No one would say that."

"What do we have for lunch?"

"Lots of protein. I can get you something."

I peered toward the line at the counter. "I'm good. I'll decide what I want as I wait."

"You sure?"

"Yep, thank you, Janice."

My five feet, seven inches had me at a disadvantage as I approached the serving counter. While I could read the screen above with today's food choices, the counter was completely hidden by the mass of men before me. I stared at the amber of a Coopers t-shirt stretched over wide shoulders and a muscular back as I waited for the way to clear.

"Hey," a deep voice bellowed.

Bodies shifted.

I turned to find Fin a few people behind me.

"Ms. Hubbard is here," he called. "Do you animals think you could let a lady get her food?"

"Sorry."

"Hey."

The players parted, giving me a straight path to the counter.

I lifted my hands. "No, you don't have to do that. I can wait like anyone else."

"I heard you were at practice."

I recognized Malik Johnson, one of our cornerbacks. "I was. I'm trying to learn more about football operations."

"Ms. Maeve, you need to watch the defense," he said. "We're the real heroes of the game."

The men around us cheered or booed and laughed. "I will. I promise. I think I need a little longer than one practice with the offense." Then I asked, "You don't mind me watching?"

"Hell no," Malik said. "Oh, sorry."

My smile grew. "I like a good hell no. Thanks, Malik."

He motioned for me to go to the front of the line.

Once I had my lunch tray, I made my way through the waiting men.

"How did it go?" Fin asked softly.

"You didn't need to do what you did earlier. I don't need special attention."

"The practice?"

"It went well. Thank you."

Fin winked. "I never had a doubt."

"That makes one person. I need to get to my office and see what I've missed."

"I'll look for you this afternoon."

I walked away with the crazy sensation of being a college student all over again.

No, I chastised myself.

Griffin Graham walked away from me.

What we had was over.

Then why was he acting like it could start again?

CHAPTER 16

Vee

The countdown to a kickoff truly began seven days before game day. In the case of today's game, the Tennessee Titans' equipment manager collaborated a week before with the Coopers' coordinator to schedule the team's arrival to Crystal Light Stadium. Much of the run-up to the game-day schedule was determined by the NFL and not up for debate. Three days before, the playing field was tested and certified to comply with the NFL requirements on hardness, depth, evenness, and other specifics. Twenty-four hours before kickoff, all game officials were required to be in Lexington. If the visiting team was traveling by airplane, they must be in the host city no less than eighteen hours before game time.

The real countdown began four hours before kickoff.

By nine o'clock a.m., Crystal Light Stadium was a beehive of activity. As vice president of stadium operations, I had a team of football operations professionals that oversaw the specifics. From the owner's suite high in the end zone, the different operations took on the appearance of a finely choreographed dance.

Today, I was witnessing the performance from the sidelines and in awe of our ops team.

Outside the stadium, the parking lots opened for tailgating. Fans began lining up to enter as much as six hours prior to game time. Inside, at the four-hour mark, the field was once again inspected, thoroughly walked to determine if it still complied with NFL regulations. Local game-day assistants arrived and began setting up their equipment and systems. The wireless communication between coaches and players (C2P) was assessed. Field technicians set up field-monitor systems. It took hundreds of people behind the scenes to pull off a precisely timed kickoff.

Two hours and fifteen minutes prior to play, each team provided twelve primary and twelve backup like-new Wilson official NFL footballs to the referee for inspection. Kicking balls received directly from Wilson Sporting Goods were also available to be inspected by one representative from each team. All the balls contained a coin-sized RFID chip that transmitted data on the ball's location, speed, spin, and trajectory. That information was used for broadcasting and later for analytics.

Two hours before, the gates to Crystal Light Stadium opened, allowing people inside. Our ushers were not only monitoring each guest, but making sure each attendee felt appreciated, passing out buttons to first-time visitors and aiding with questions. At the same time, final testing was done with each team's equipment managers to assure the C2P systems were working properly.

Nothing was overlooked.

Communication between all medical staff—local league-appointed neurotrauma consultants, airway management physician, emergency response physician, and athletic trainer spotters—was evaluated. The AT spotters were certified athletic trainers stationed in the stadium booth to help each team's medical staff spot potential concussion or other head and neck injuries.

All printing and Microsoft Surface tablets were in place on the sidelines.

An hour and forty minutes prior to kickoff was the security meeting, attended by the referee, league and team security representatives, NFL football operations representative, stadium security, local senior public safety official, and often an FBI representative. Keeping our fans safe was a top priority.

Ninety minutes prior to kickoff, there was an officiating meeting that included both teams' PR directors, sideline communications, NFL sideline TV coordinator, NFL football operations representative, the TV network representative, the network's on-field communications coordinator, and the seven-person officiating team. During this meeting, broadcast policies and procedures were discussed. Game Day Administration Reports—including each team's inactive list, players designated to have C2P components in their helmets, and players/coaches wearing microphones—were presented.

Watches were also synchronized—the countdown was continuing.

By one hour before kickoff, the roof at Crystal Light Stadium was either opened or closed; it couldn't change after that deadline. Today, it was open. This was also the time when both teams were allowed onto the field for warm-up and practice. Officials also entered the field. Each team had half the field for this workout.

If the entire process was a symphony, at this point, the conductor would increase the tempo, bringing the fever within the stadium to the much-anticipated crescendo. In-house football ops working in tandem with the NFL, ESPN, or whichever broadcasting system, and the dozens of coaches, nearly a hundred players, worked tirelessly to give the effortless appearance to the seventy thousand fans in the stadium as well as the hundreds of thousands of TV viewers.

It was truly a scripted musical composition.

As the vice president of stadium operations, I had complete faith in my team. Today's nerves weren't due to the climactic lead-up. They were tightening my skin and increasing my rapid heartbeat due to my location —not safely in the family suite but on the sideline, in the middle of the mayhem.

This was our first regular season game. During the preseason, the Coopers won two of our three games. A sold-out crowd was filling Crystal Light Stadium in anticipation of today's game against the Titans.

Our roster was now down to the mandatory forty-eight active players, with sixteen players on the practice squad. We had a solid team. While Fin received playing time during preseason, now was the time for Troy Dennison to shine.

The view of Crystal Light from the sideline was completely different than it was up in the family suite. I peered upward, squinting through my sunglasses as a sea of amber filled the seats. Lexington's blue sky shone above the stadium through the opened roof.

At the one-hour mark while the team was out on the field warming up, I asked Drew my nagging question. "Are you sure I won't be in the way?"

"Vee, you've been to every offense practice session for the last two weeks. You've heard the plays. You know what's supposed to happen. Unlike practice, the real game has obstacles. Listen when I call the plays. Then watch to see if they're played out. If they are, notice what went right. If they're not, figure out where they went wrong." His cheeks rose with a smile. "It's a whole new world with an opposing team, a packed stadium, and an officiating crew."

"Okay. Thank you."

"Make notes. There's no time to discuss during the game. Tomorrow we'll talk about what you saw."

I returned his smile. "Drew, thank you for being welcoming to me. You remind me of Roy Everington. He tried to include me."

"Best compliment I've heard today." He patted my shoulder.

Standing behind the white paint, I walked up and down the field, noticing the different team of technicians, identified by the color of their hats. Yellow, orange, purple, blue, and gray were hurriedly doing their assigned tasks.

The suspense grew as pregame announcements came over the PA system. The countdown clock was ticking as the visiting Tennessee Titans took the field. High above, the seats were filled and fans were screaming. The PA system roared with AC/DC *Thunderstruck* as fireworks shot from the four corners of the stadium.

Our home-team announcer, the Big Hurt, spoke in his signature commanding tone. "Ladies and gentlemen, your Lexington Coopers."

Applause and cheering erupted, the decibels reaching a fevered pitch.

My pulse increased as fog emanated from the dark tunnel, and the Coopers, dressed in their amber game-day jerseys, ran onto the field. The special effects manufactured by strobing lights and a fog machine created the appearance of crackling electricity around the players. The Big Hurt named the starting offense player by player, including their college affiliation, and then the same for the starting defense.

Goose bumps prickled my skin as the excitement built. I wasn't sure why I'd never thought to be on the sidelines before, but the thrill made me wonder if I could go back to the family suite, six stories above.

Troy Dennison was out on the field with Kai Flores, our cornerback, and two Titans players for the coin toss. The referee's voice billowed as the image of the five people filled the jumbotron.

"As the visiting team," the head official said to the Titans' quarterback, "you get to choose heads or tails."

"We choose heads."

The referee tossed the coin into the air, allowing it to land on the field. "Tails." He turned to Troy. "What do you want to do?"

"We'll defer."

The referee repeated Troy's answer for the crowd to hear. "The Coopers will defer."

More screams and cheers reverberate throughout the stadium.

The Coopers' kicking team would be on the field first. I looked down at my watch as the special team came forward. It was exactly 12:59 p.m. The ops team came through.

Now was time for the football players to show the world we were contenders. The clock struck one o'clock p.m. and our kicker sent the football into the air. The Titans signaled for a fair catch.

It was time for our defense to take the field.

The defensive coordinator's calls came through my earpiece. Darius's calls weren't all that different from Drew's. While I didn't have time to decipher their meaning, the language and cadence were similar. I soon realized his calls often changed once he saw the Titan offense lined up.

Four and out.

The Titans punted.

Time for our offense.

From my point of view, I saw Fin slap Troy's shoulder pad as Troy ran onto the field.

A smile curled my lips. While I hadn't wanted Fin to be a part of the Coopers, maybe I'd been wrong. Maybe Fin truly could be happy as a mentor to Troy and playing second string.

The first half ended with the Coopers up seventeen to ten.

We were the first team to receive the ball as the second half began. A high kick, and our special teams ran the ball to the Coopers' forty-two-yard line. Fantastic field position as our offense took the field.

Drew's call came through loud and clear.

I watched as the ball was snapped. Troy faked a handoff to the fullback Treshawn Morgan. Our running back, Dijon Ortiz, also tucked a make-believe ball. The two backs took off, decoys. Troy stepped back, reading his receivers.

The defense had all the possible receivers covered.

Tucking the ball, Troy ran forward. The defense was closing in.

Troy slid, getting the Coopers near seven yards on the play.

The crowd cheered.

A collective gasp filled the air as the Titans' linebacker charged, plowing into Troy after he was already in his slide.

"Late hit," the angry call came from the players on the sideline.

Flags flew.

The referees blew their whistles. My heart pounded in my chest.

Troy was still down.

"Troy, get up," I whispered as I turned my attention

to the replay on the jumbotron. It showed what we'd all witnessed; Troy ran and slid. The linebacker came flying, hitting Troy with a forearm to the head and neck, their helmets colliding as Troy's neck snapped forward, before snapping back and landing hard on the turf.

The Coopers' players on the sideline were furious. The coaching team and assistants worked to keep the enraged teammates from entering the field.

Tilson and Drew ran with the medical team to Troy.

Troy was still down.

CHAPTER 17

Fin

The entire sidelines stood, everyone, ready to take the field. We couldn't look away from Troy Dennison. "Move," I said under my breath. "Damn it, move," I screamed louder.

My yells were part of a chorus as the entire team's screams turned to silence.

The medical personnel as well as Coach Tilson and Pratt were on the field. The Coopers' offense was now kneeling in a circle around our star player. Crystal Light Stadium that had seconds ago been roaring was now deadly silent as everyone watched. The cameras were no longer on Dennison. With the wall of players, we couldn't see a thing. As someone reached for my hand, I turned, looking down field.

The players on the sidelines were now kneeling. I joined them. My gaze went to the woman on the sidelines. Vee stood with her hands clenched to her chest. It was the shattered look of helplessness that stuck like a knife in my chest.

Troy Dennison was the Coopers' miracle. A first-round draft pick from Alabama, last season he outplayed all the predictions. The kid was only twenty-three years old. I closed my eyes.

The ring of cheers and applause caused me to open my eyes and stand.

Troy was on a long stretcher, his neck and head braced. The camera caught him lifting his hand and waving at the crowd. The relief was overwhelming. I turned once again toward Vee, seeing her wipe her cheeks.

"Fin," Coach Garcia, the quarterback coach, screamed. "You're in."

Teammates slapped my shoulder pads. "Fuck them."

"Make them pay."

"You've got this."

Their words were the sparks igniting a fire within me. I'd wanted a few more years. Taking the job with the Coopers was supposed to be my firsthand view to budding greatness. That was my opinion of Dennison. The kid had the potential of a Hall-of-Famer written all over him.

Over the last few weeks, he and I had worked out after practice because Garcia wanted us to. Tuesday mornings, we worked out together because we wanted to. I might be the veteran, but during those moments with only the two of us in the workout room, we both shared our knowledge, our advice, and our secrets to success.

The ruling on the field had been roughing the passer. Pickard, the Titan linebacker, was ejected with possible suspensions. Unnecessary roughness resulted in a fifteen-yard penalty and an automatic first down. That put our line of scrimmage on the Titans' thirty-yard line.

Drew spoke, facing me, his lips hidden from cameras. Holding on to my shoulder pads, he screamed, "We're within field-goal range. Holt can make a forty-seven-yard attempt." He shook his head. "I don't want to play prevent here." His smile grew. "Show the world what Griffin Graham can do. Show LA they were wrong to keep you on the bench. Go."

The offense ran onto the field.

We huddled.

I gave the call. Instead of break, I yelled, "For Dennison."

We lined up in split-back formation. The Titans' defense shifted, preparing for the run play. I called out the play again, with a slight change, running an RPO—run pass option. The sons-of-bitches were expecting us to run. They thought by bringing down Dennison, they brought down the Coopers' passing game.

I set the cadence. "Set, hut!"

The ball was snapped from center. I stepped back, reading my progressions. Our offensive guards and tackles were giving me time. I fake passed to Morgan, our full back. He took off. The defense took the bait. I looked down field. JD was wide open. My arm went back.

The grasp and throw were second nature. I let it rip.

As soon as the ball left my hand, I was tackled.

There were no fucks I had to give. Brushing the defender off, I sat up in time to see JD with the catch in the endzone.

Fireworks spouted from the stadium as the crowd screamed.

"Good job, Fin," came from inside my helmet.

As we ran off the field, I turned away from the coaches and peered where Vee had been. The tears she'd shed for Dennison were gone, replaced by a beautiful smile.

"Any word on Troy?" I asked Coach Garcia as our extra-point special team took the field.

"Concussion protocol," he said. "We'll know more after the docs do their thing. He's moving all extremities. You're in for the rest of the game."

For Dennison became our mantra. The Coopers' defense was on fire. Going into the final two minutes of the game, the score was thirty-one Coopers to nineteen, Titans. They'd been held to field goals.

Miscommunications with our kicking team unexpectedly had a Titan rushing eighty-seven yards for a touchdown. Within only seconds, we were now only up by six. The Titan offense went back on the field trying for a two-point conversion.

Crystal Light Stadium was the loudest I'd ever heard. The fans were as rabid as the players on the field. A chant came from the stands— "For Dennison. For Dennison."

Our defense held.

"Offense, prevent, offense. Use the clock," Drew said. "We don't want to let them back on the field."

The first two plays our offensive line created holes. The backs made three yards and five yards respectively. We were now third down and two. The play in my ear was for another run. As we lined up in split formation, I scanned the defense. Their cornerbacks were tight. I called another RPO.

The ball was snapped.

I read my progression.

JD Downing was covered.

Kylon Lewis, one wide receiver was blocked.

Ramel Patel, our other wide receiver was open.

I threw the ball.

Patel caught the ball on the Titan's forty-seven-yard line. Patel was tackled, staying in bounds. The clock kept ticking. The next play was a run play. We needed one more first down to run out the clock.

On second down, I threw the ball to Morgan who went wide left. It was now third down and one. The ball was snapped. I held on and ran, Morgan and Bennett tush-pushed behind me.

"First down," came from the speakers above.

The Titans had a timeout remaining, but so did we.

The game was over.

Coopers won.

Tilson met me at the sidelines. "Tomorrow we're going to talk."

I could have argued my case for not following the play call, but experience told me to wait, wait for tomorrow. We'd know more about Troy by then and cooler heads would hopefully prevail.

Vee was standing near the tunnel after I'd had a chance to be interviewed by a few of the broadcasters on the field.

Her smile was stunning. "Good game, Graham."

"And you didn't want me here."

She tilted her head. "I can admit when I'm wrong. Can you?"

Morgan slapped my shoulder pads. "Get in here, Fin."

When I turned, Vee was gone.

CHAPTER 18

Vee

When the elevator door opened on the sixth floor, I was face-to-face with my cousin Leigh and her husband, Hayden.

"Vee," she said loudly as she wrapped her arms around me. "Oh my God. That game was crazy."

"What do we know about Troy?" I asked.

Leigh sighed. "Pickard, the Titans' linebacker, is out for three additional games. Uncle Reid has been talking with people from the NFL office."

"It was a late hit. Targeted." I looked toward the family suite. "Is my dad still here?"

"Yeah. He's been on the phone a lot since Dennison went out."

There were more questions I wanted to ask, but Dad would be the one who could give me the answers. We said our goodbyes as they went to the elevator, and I nodded to a familiar usher. He opened the door for me. Despite the game having been over for nearly half an hour, the suite was still filled with people.

I was caught short at the sight of Preston.

"Vee."

"You came? I told you I wouldn't be up here."

Wrapping his arm around my waist, he led me away from the rest of the family. His dark stare met mine. "I was hoping you'd come up during the game."

"Drew Pratt invited me to the sidelines." The earlier excitement returned. "It was amazing. I'd never really watched my ops teams in action, not from that close. And the energy in the air was palpable. It was as if there was electricity. And having an earpiece was so different than during practices. I'm getting better at the plays, but everything is faster during a game—like practice on steroids."

Preston's expression was filled with questions.

"Vee," Dad said, coming up behind me. "Have you heard about Troy?"

My expression morphed. "No. How is he?"

"Has a concussion. They're doing more scans. The doctors are also concerned with a sprained neck."

"Injured reserve?" I asked.

Dad shook his head. "Not yet. We have to make a decision by tomorrow."

If Dennison was placed on the IR, he would be out of at least four games. "Maybe we should think about calling Simpson back."

"He's on New Orleans's practice team."

"Vee," Uncle Darin said, "we've talked about it. We know what we're doing."

"Simpson knows the calls," I said. I turned to Dad. "You wanted me to learn more about football operations. I've spent the last two weeks with the offense."

"And now," Grant said, walking up to us, "she's an expert."

My attention was on my dad. "I'm not an expert. I'm practical. If Dennison goes on injured reserve, there's no one to back Fin. We need a backup."

"You were on the sidelines?" Grant asked, swirling what looked like whiskey in his tumbler. "You're carrying this a little too far, don't you think?"

"Drew asked if I wanted to be there. I said yes."

"For publicity's sake, I hope it was a one and done."

"I don't know," Dad interjected. "Vee, if being close to the action was something you enjoyed—did you enjoy it?"

I let out a long sigh. "It was incredible."

Dad turned to Grant. "You've always had that option. Just because you didn't take advantage of the experience doesn't mean Vee should pass it up." He reached for my arm. "Observing. No micromanaging. No play calling."

I laughed. "I'm definitely not calling plays." I started to comment about the play where Fin was supposed to have one of his backs run for short yardage, but instead he threw to Patel for a first down and then some, but I doubted anyone up in the suite was aware of the change. After all, Fin's play worked.

"I don't see any harm in Vee standing field side."

Preston joined the discussion. "Does that mean you'll be traveling with the team to Denver next week?"

"Not with the team," I said. "But yes, I'll travel to Denver." I turned to Dad. "Are you going?"

"Yes. You can fly with Daphne and me."

Daphne, yay.

I looked at Preston. "You're welcome to come along. Just know that during the game, I'll be on the sidelines."

"I'll have to think about that invitation." He tilted his head toward the bar. "How about a drink? Have you eaten?"

"Not since early this morning." I looked at what remained of the food on the buffet and wrinkled my nose. "One cosmo for tradition's sake."

Once the red cocktail was in front of me, Preston spoke softly, "How about we go back to my place. It's a beautiful day. I'll grill chicken and corn. We can relax.

You've been working too hard lately, studying plays every night. You deserve a night off."

Lifting my glass, I took a sip and opened my eyes wide. "Strong."

"Then I'll drive."

I met Preston's stare. "That sounds inviting."

His neck straightened. "You're going to decline."

Looking around, I scanned the remaining family and lowered my voice. "Dad wants me to understand the football side of the Coopers better. I'm also juggling all my regular work. Depending on when Dad and Daphne want to fly to Denver, I'm probably looking at a shortened workweek."

He clenched his jaw. "I thought if I came here today, you'd realize we've hardly spent any time together in weeks."

"It hasn't been that long."

"I promised you a date after returning from Bowling Green."

"I'm sorry." I shook my head. "No, I'm not."

"What?"

"I'm not going to your place, and you're not coming to mine. Why can't you be happy for me?"

"Happy that you're working yourself sick?" Preston questioned.

"This extra work doesn't feel like work. I tried to tell you how exhilarating it was to be down on the sideline. You didn't say a word."

"I didn't have a chance. Reid joined the conversation."

Turning, I met his gaze and squared my shoulders. "Here's your chance."

"For what?"

"To reply to what I told you earlier."

Preston ran his hand over his hair. "Fuck, I don't remember." His nostrils flared. "I'm glad you're excited and exhilarated. I wish you felt that way about me."

One more sip.

Forgetting that, I tipped the glass back, swallowing the remaining cocktail, and set it on the bar. "You know what?" I stared into the hazel of his eyes, seeing the golden flecks that used to intrigue me. "I wish I did too."

"What the fuck are you saying?" he growled near my ear.

"I'm saying, thanks, Preston, for finally making it clear. Right now, I need some space to learn what's involved with the Coopers—the whole franchise—things that I've previously overlooked."

"Fucking breaking up with me in the goddamned family suite?"

"Would it have been better to wait until we were at your place?"

Preston reached for my hand. "At least there I could try to convince you otherwise."

I shook my head. "I'm beyond convincing." I called the bartender. "One more cosmo, please."

Preston looked from side to side and stepped away from the barstool. "Call me if you decide you have time in your life for me."

I didn't reply; instead, I stared up at the TV screen. Thankfully, the closed captioning was on. The reporter was showing the hit on Dennison. Seeing it again made me squirm. The broadcast team at the table were discussing his injury and predictions on his possible return.

"Oh shit," Lip said, taking the seat Preston had just left as my new drink arrived.

I turned, meeting his expression. "Shit what?" I questioned as I blinked away unexpected tears.

Lip put his arm around me.

I laid my head on his shoulder.

"He wasn't good enough for you."

Looking up, I grinned. "He's thoroughbred royalty."

Lip moved his arm. "Oh, that's right. I'm sure the Clarks and Preston himself thought he was too good, but he wasn't." Lip wrinkled his nose. "The man was a little too cocky with nothing to show for it but Daddy's money." Lip lifted his chin.

I followed his line of vision to see Fin, showered and sitting at the press briefing.

"Now, Fin may be cocky," Lip said, "but from what I've seen, he's riding on his own talent, not old money."

He wiggled his eyebrows. "It's been a bit, but do you remember just how cocky he is?"

Shaking my head, I closed my eyes as warmth filled my cheeks. "Fourteen years is a long time." That didn't mean I didn't remember. It meant I didn't want to discuss it.

"I'd guess the size hasn't changed," Lip said softly, "but the art of delivery has no doubt improved with practice."

Staring up at the TV, I noticed a bruise blooming on Fin's left cheek and a small bandage on his forehead. "I don't know."

"He came here to the Coopers knowing you were part of the franchise."

"He also left me. He never called when he said he would. I even reached out."

"How many times?" Lip asked.

I shrugged and swallowed. "A few. Each time was more humiliating than the last."

"Ask him."

Lifting my hands, I rubbed my temples. A dull thumping was growing louder. "I should go home."

"I'll drive you."

The staff was cleaning and taking down the buffet. "I'll grab a dry chicken sandwich. That should soak up the vodka."

"Chris and I are meeting downtown for dinner tonight. Why don't you join us?"

I stood from the barstool and feigned a smile. "Thanks. I don't want to be a third wheel."

"You wouldn't be. Besides, you're my favorite cousin."

It was something I'd said to Grant.

"I'm your only cousin." There were now fewer people in the suite. "Why don't you invite him here for games?"

"Yeah, I'm not ready for that."

"When you are, I'll be here for you."

Lip tilted his head. "You better be on the sideline. I saw how excited you were when you entered the suite. Keep that enthusiasm going." He stood. "Are you okay?"

"Two-year itch. It needed to be scratched."

"More like a crusty scab on your ass." My cousin grinned. "And now it's gone."

Leaning closer, I gave Lip a hug. "Thank you."

"Leigh will be thrilled," he whispered.

One more look up at the TV. Fin was gone. The Titans' coach was seated, discussing Pickard's suspension.

CHAPTER 19

Vee

It was nearly six in the evening when I pulled into the parking garage beneath the Vine, the building in the heart of downtown Lexington. After graduating from college, I moved into a downtown apartment. A couple of years later, after I broke up with Kelcee or maybe it was Josh, I decided I wanted something more stable, something that was mine.

My three-bedroom and three-and-a-half-bath condominium had plenty of room to grow. As I exited my car, I realized that growing wasn't something I was ready to do. I obviously didn't want to leave my condo to live with Preston. However, when given the chance, I didn't want him to move in with me either.

Waiting for the elevator, I closed my eyes.

Recent reports on Troy Dennison were promising. He was awake, talking, and moving. The doors opened, and I passed my key card over the sensor and hit seven, for the seventh floor. The doors closed. My reflection in the golden doors wasn't filled with the excitement I had earlier this morning. My thoughts went to a hot bubble bath and a glass of wine.

The doors opened on the first floor.

As neighbors I recognized but didn't know their names entered, beyond them I saw a familiar face. He stood a head taller than those around him. Without thinking, I pushed my way out of the elevator.

Fin.

The first floor of the Vine contained a bar, the Vine Club, and a five-star restaurant.

Was Fin on a date?

While I knew I had no reason to know the answer to that question or to be jealous, my rational brain was sinking in a concoction of play calls and post-breakup blues. I followed a few steps behind, trying to figure out if Fin was alone, with a date, or a group.

Inconspicuously, I moved with a group of women as they passed the entrance to the Vine Club. Through the large archway, I spotted Fin standing near the bar next to...

I blinked.

I knew the man at his side.

Zane Graham.

Fin's younger brother.

A smile curled my lips as relief flooded my circulation. Fin met his brother after the game. As my headache returned, I turned around and headed toward the elevators.

"Vee."

"No. Shit." I ducked my head and continued on my way.

As I stopped for the elevator, a large hand grasped my arm. Turning, I met Fin's blue gaze.

"Vee, what are you doing here?" he asked.

I looked up at the blossoming bruise on his cheek that did nothing to dull his sexy smile. "I live here." I jutted my chin. "I'm going up to my place."

"I didn't know that. Do you remember Zane?"

Stupidly, I shook my head before saying, "Oh yeah. Your little brother."

Fin laughed. "Younger. He's taller and outweighs me. He came to Lexington for the game."

A smile came to my lips. "He got to see you play."

"It was a gamble. I warned him." Small lines crinkled near his eyes. "We're in the bar. Why don't you join us?"

I scanned Fin from his leather loafers to his gelled hair as a cloud of sandalwood filled my senses. "I'm..."

I looked down and back up. My clothes were wrinkled, and I probably smelled from perspiring in the sun. "I haven't had a chance to clean up or change since the game. I should—"

"It's only a drink. Zane would love to see you."

Air filled my lungs as I inhaled. "Tonight's not a good night."

Fin's expression sobered. "I've spoken to Troy."

"You have?"

"He'll be all right."

"How long will he be out?" I asked.

"They're doing more tests. The coaches should know by tomorrow." He quirked his smile. "Come on, join us. Tell us what you thought of the sidelines. Your expressions made me think you were having the time of your life."

"How could you see me while playing?"

He shrugged. "I took peeks when I could."

The time of my life.

Why couldn't Preston recognize that?

I reached up and gently touched the bruise under his left eye and then the bandage on his forehead. "What happened?"

He scoffed. "You might not have noticed, but big men kept knocking me down."

"I did see that."

"One drink," he said.

"One."

Fin and I walked together within the crowd of people. When we turned the corner, Zane waved from a stool at the bar. As we got closer, it appeared he'd secured one other stool to his side.

"You can sit," Fin said, pulling out the stool. "I'll stand so this old body doesn't stiffen up."

As I took the seat, Zane turned in my direction. He'd grown up since I last saw him, resembling his brother even more today than he had fourteen years earlier. Of course, the last time I saw him, he was in high school. "Vee, damn, it's good to see you."

"Zane, what have you been up to?"

Fin patted Zane's shoulder. "My brother's the starting center for the Vikings."

That explained his added bulk.

My eyes opened wide. "No. How did I not know that?"

Zane brought his hands to his chest. "I had the biggest crush on you when you two were together. Now I'm crushed that you haven't been following my career."

"Give her a break," Fin said. "She's working on her own career."

"Were you on the sidelines today?" Zane asked.

"I was. How did you know?"

"They showed you a few times on the jumbotron with your name, and I thought, damn, she's even more beautiful than I remember."

While my cheeks warmed at his compliment, my neck stiffened. "I'll be having words with our camera crew."

"I think it's cool," Zane said.

"So do I," Fin replied. "What did you think?"

"May I get you a drink?" the bartender, a thin man with tattoos on his neck and fingers, asked.

"A cosmo, please."

Fin grinned. "I remember a time you swore off vodka for the rest of your life."

"Don't remind me," I groaned. The vodka had been in screwdrivers. I'd sworn off orange juice too.

"Tell us," Fin said, "what you thought."

Our gaze met. "If I ask you something, will you tell me the truth?"

"Always."

"On the last drive, on third down, did I misunderstand Drew's play?"

Fin grinned. "What do you mean?"

"I thought he called for a run play."

"Damn, Vee. You're right. He did. Patel was open, and I wasn't sure we'd get the first down with the way the defensive line was coming at our backs." He nodded. "Tilson has promised to chew my ass Monday about that."

I lifted my cosmo and winked. "It was a good play. You saved the game."

"I told you," Zane said.

Fin lifted his beer mug and our glasses clinked.

I was sipping my second cosmo, and the three of us were talking Coopers and Vikings when a buzzer on the bar began to vibrate.

Fin lifted the buzzer. "Our table is ready." His expression softened. "Join Zane and me for dinner."

"No. You have a table for two." I downed the last of my cosmo. "There's a bubble bath calling me. I need to go upstairs."

"You live here?" Zane asked.

"I do."

Fin took my glass from my grasp. "I think it's a good thing you're not driving. Zane can get our table, and I'll walk you to your place."

A laugh bubbled from my lips. "Chivalry isn't dead."

Fin offered me his hand.

CHAPTER 20

Vee

The bar and patrons faded, and my world wobbled as I laid my hand in Fin's. Perhaps the few bites of a dry chicken sandwich weren't sufficient to counteract the potency of four cosmos. "Thank you." I eased myself down from the barstool. "I can make it upstairs fine on my own."

"I could pick you up and carry you."

I attributed the way his threat made my heart beat in double time to the alcohol. A scan of his handsome features searched for a sign of jest and came up empty. "Wouldn't that make the *Lexington Herald*? Maeve Hubbard and current first-string quarterback, Griffin Graham..."

Fin tipped his head toward Zane.

"I'll get the table," his brother said, standing and walking away.

A strong arm wrapped around me. "What floor?"

"Seven." I sighed, allowing Fin to lead me out of the bar and back toward the elevators. My mind swirled with the happenings of the day. The range of emotions from anxiousness to elation to fear, and to...I wasn't sure what to label my breakup, the jumbled mix with a lack of nourishment had me totally drained.

As we stopped for the elevator, I pulled away from Fin's arm. I could stand on my own. Crossing my arms over my chest, I asked, "Do you think Troy will be all right?"

"He's young and strong. He'll be all right. I just don't want him to come back sooner than he should. I've seen that happen too many times."

The doors opened.

We stood silently as the elevator emptied. Together, we stepped in. I reached into my bag and pulled out my keycard.

Fin took it from my grasp, placed it over the sensor, and pushed the button for seven.

"I could have made it home."

His sexy lips quirked. "I have no doubt, Ms. Hubbard, that you can do anything you set your mind to."

When the doors opened, I led the way down the

hallway. My condo was the last door on the left—a corner unit with two walls of windows and a wrap-around balcony.

My tongue darted to my lips as we reached my condo. "We made it. Thank you, Mr. Graham." I reached into my tote for my keycard.

Like a magician, Fin produced the card from his hand and placed it over the sensor. The light turned green as the locking mechanism whirled. Turning the knob, he pushed my door inward. The humming was my reminder to enter the security code.

The temperature rose as we both stared into the darkened condo, lit only by the dusk sky through the floor-to-ceiling windows, and turned back to one another. I stepped inside, entering the code on the keypad. Instead of stepping away, Fin stood in the doorway unmoving, his sandalwood scent tickling my senses and his muscular body close enough to touch. The urge to lift my arms over Fin's shoulders and press my body against his was overwhelming. My alcohol-soaked mind tried to speak reason, but my body was pretending not to hear.

"Zane's waiting," I finally said.

"Vee." His deep baritone rendition of my name ricocheted through me.

Lip's advice came back, a reminder to ask Fin why he didn't return my calls.

I couldn't form the words, scared to face his answer.

Not today.

Not after Troy's injury.

Not after Preston.

"I should—" My words were stopped as Fin lifted my chin and brought his strong lips to mine. The electricity in his kiss short-circuited my thoughts. My arms moved upward to his wide shoulders. My fingers wove through his soft dark hair at the nape of his neck.

In some magical trance, we were now both inside my apartment, no longer in the hallway. The door closed. I gave no resistance as Fin's kiss continued, his tongue sought entrance as he pressed his solid body against mine. His fingers splayed beneath my top, caging my ribs. The moans filling the air were coming from me.

I gasped as all at once, my hands were above my head, pinned to the wall above me. Fin's handsome face was before me, his thumb rubbing seductively over my lower lip, and the taste of his beer on my tongue. Overstimulation had my nerves stretched taut. I longed to touch him, to run my fingers over his muscular body that had matured to perfection.

Fin towered above me, dwarfing me in his presence. Yet there was no fear. The emotions running rapidly through me were a potent mixture of wanton desire and stupidity. This was the last thing we should be doing.

My attempts to free my wrists were futile as Fin continued his laser-focused stare of me.

"Damn, Vee. I've fucking missed you." His deep voice rattled my core.

It was as if my tongue had forgotten how to speak. The construction of words seemed out of the question; sentences were impossible. All I could do was stare into his sapphire orbs, now mostly black.

The centers of his eyes were dilated in the dim light or was it something else, was it the kaleidoscope of yearning simmering in the blue ring surrounding his enlarged pupils?

With his hand that wasn't keeping an iron grip of my wrists, Fin's forefinger trailed from my cheek, lower to my neck and collarbone, each inch the striking of steel over flint, leaving goose bumps in its wake. His touch was a match lighting flames to dry underbrush. The resulting forest fire threatened catastrophic consequences.

Fin released my wrists, only to secure them again at my sides.

The distance between us disappeared as his massive frame pressed against my smaller one. Chest to chest, his heartbeat vibrated from him to me, sending shock waves throughout my circulation. His erection probed my stomach, confirming that my wants weren't one-sided.

This was the Fin I remembered.

The unabashed dominant lover.

The only man who had ever shown me what truly trusting another soul could do, the walls it could demolish and the ecstasies it could unleash, his abilities morphed into a curse over time. It was like drinking Dom Perignon as my first taste of champagne and then spending the rest of my life searching through grocery store shelves for anything remotely close and only finding cheap imitations.

The lust-filled fog cleared.

Fin released my wrists.

I lifted a palm to his sternum and pushed, moving him a smidgen away. Beneath my touch of his rock-hard chest, his heart also raced. "Fin."

He took a step back, ran his palm over his face. His fingers raked through his dark hair. "Vee, I'm sorry."

I shook my head. "Don't apologize. Today has been..."

"You're seeing Preston. I have no right..."

It seemed completing sentences was now an inability we both shared. "I broke it off with him today."

Fin's gaze locked onto mine. "You did?"

"Yeah. Leigh says I have commitment issues."

His lips quirked. "I recall someone saying the same thing about me—and my commitment to a team."

Exhaling, I straightened my top and smiled. "Have a nice dinner with Zane."

"Zane. Fuck."

Turning, I walked to the door and opened it. "I'm sure we'll see one another. Let's not mention this."

"I want to fucking scream it from the fifty-yard line." He stepped into the hallway.

"You played great today, Fin. I'm glad you're on our team."

Fin nodded.

I remembered something else. "What you asked earlier, about the sidelines..." I nodded. "I was having the time of my life. I guess this day has been a whirlwind of emotions."

While Fin looked as if he was about to reply, I closed the door. As soon as it was locked, I rubbed my sore wrists, leaned against the door, and sighed. I didn't even realize my cheeks were damp with tears until I made my way through the large empty condo toward my bedroom, more accurately, my garden tub.

My bubble bath was calling.

CHAPTER 21

Fin

Monday morning, I stuffed my shit into my locker space before making my way to the film room. Akin to a movie theater, the large film room had enough seats for the entire team. That wasn't where I was supposed to be. My stop would be in the offensive film review, a smaller theater room down the hallway. Entering near the back, my gaze met offensive coordinator Drew Pratt's. He offered me a clipped nod.

Did he know about Tilson wanting to speak to me?

His expression only said to take a seat.

The room filled as Coach Tilson, Coach Garcia, and the other offensive-position coaches congregated in the front of the room. Without appearing obvious, I searched for any sign of Vee. The sight of her vivid green eyes and the taste of her sweet lips from last night were on repeat in my dreams. Waking didn't seem to slow the memories. If I thought about the way she moaned when I spread my fingers over her soft skin beneath her top, I'd get hard in a room full of testosterone.

Corden Young, an offensive tackle, took the seat to my side. He had six years in the league, and this was his third with the Coopers. "Good game, yesterday."

"Thanks for keeping me safe."

Corden scoffed. "That shiner you're sporting doesn't look like we did that good of a job."

Gingerly, I lifted my fingers to my cheek, below my left eye. "Looks worse than it feels."

The seats were filling as he lowered his voice. "News about Dennison?"

Pressing my lips together, I shook my head. "Nothing since yesterday. I spoke to him after the news conference. He sounded positive. I'm sure they're going to let us know."

A hand came to my shoulder from behind. A quick crane of my neck and I saw JD's smile. "Good to work together again."

JD's light green eyes contrasted with his dark complexion. It was his constant smile and ready laugh that I'd missed. "Missed you, too. I'm here until Dennison can take back his place."

"Quiet," Coach Tilson said from the front. "The injury report hasn't been finalized yet." He lifted his hand to keep us quiet. "I know everyone's wondering about Dennison. The official diagnosis is a grade-one concussion and neck sprain." His eyes came to me. "Fin will be starting next Sunday in Denver."

It was difficult to describe the feeling registering in my gut.

I'd be lying if I didn't like hearing my name on the starting lineup. On the other hand, this was my thirteenth season in the NFL. I'd been mowed down by some of the league's best defensive players. The ache in my body as I woke this morning told me that I was meant to step aside for the younger and healthier class.

"The Coopers' plane will leave Thursday afternoon an hour after practice ends. Be ready. We don't wait. As our veterans know, they don't call Denver 'mile-high stadium' for nothing. Stadium ops have worked out two days of practice in Denver to get you used to breathing the thinner air. Now, we're not going to spend a lot of time rewatching Packard's hit on Troy. I would, however, like us to watch one time, not to analyze the hit, but to look at our O line. Could we have prevented it?"

Corden bristled and murmured under his breath.

"The hit was late," Drew Pratt interjected. "We're

not assigning blame. Packard shouldn't have been still targeting. If any of you guards or tackles had stopped him, you would have been called for a late hit. Nevertheless, this is an opportunity for us to evaluate the possibilities."

When the film review of the game was over, I headed to Coach Tilson's office. "The coach wanted to see me, Griffin Graham," I said to his assistant.

She picked up the phone. When she hung up, she shook her head. "Coach Tilson is busy right now and said not to worry about it. Everything worked out."

"All right." Turning, I let out a breath.

Cooler minds.

It was around eleven when I made my way to the trainer's office. Turning each corner, I hoped to run into a green-eyed beauty. Either she was avoiding me or our paths weren't meant to cross. I suspected the first and hoped for the second. Not crossing paths was easier to remedy.

"How are you feeling, Fin?" Lacy Reynolds asked as I entered the exam room.

I met Lacy my first week with the Coopers. She was a certified athletic trainer and a physician's assistant. In her mid-fifties, Lacy had been with the Coopers since they moved to Crystal Light Stadium.

"Sorer than I'd like to admit."

She hummed and nodded. "Where? Besides that left cheek."

"Everywhere," I said, hoping to be funny. By the look on her face, I saw my attempt at humor wasn't hitting its mark. "I soaked in the hot tub this morning before our meeting. I just wondered if you had any other recommendations."

Lacy asked me to lie down on one of the tables. After I did, she began her examination. The nylon shorts I was wearing gave her access to my calves and thighs. Pushing and kneading the muscles and tendons in my legs and hips, she asked, "How are your ribs—your sides?"

"Good." I took off my shirt, pulling it over my head, and she examined me for bruises and tenderness.

I groaned as she kneaded my right shoulder. "Tender?"

"A little."

"We should get an MRI."

"I'd rather not."

Lacy took a step back and crossed her arms. "That's not how this works. I'm not asking."

Sitting up, I swung my legs over the table and gave her my sexiest grin. "Hear me out." She lowered her arms—it was a start. "Dennison is out for at least the next game. You know more than I do." She didn't respond. "I haven't had any pain during practice, but I'd blocked out the way it feels the day after being run over by eight trucks in one afternoon. I'm good for the next game. I just wanted some suggestions on feeling better and healing quicker."

"You could have a torn—"

"Could, but I don't," I interrupted, moving my right arm in a complete windmill forward and then backward. "We don't have a third-string quarterback." I jumped to the ground, reached for my shirt, and pulled it over my head. "I'm not asking for meds, just suggestions."

Lacy pressed her lips together before sighing. "No physical activity today or tomorrow. Ice on for twenty, heat on for twenty, today and tonight. Tomorrow, heat on for twenty then nothing for twenty. If you're worse tomorrow, don't ignore it. Come in and see me. If you're not better by Wednesday morning, come to me before practice."

I quirked my grin and nodded. "Yes, ma'am."

She reached for my arm. "You're not invincible, Fin."

"Oh, do I know that."

"Playing injured doesn't help the team."

I shook my head. "I'm not injured. I'm beat up. There's a difference."

"Come back after your position meeting. I'll have a shoulder wrap for you to take home. It's both warm and cold without changing ice packs."

I agreed.

During lunch, I kept my eyes peeled for any sign of

Vee. While others from the stadium operations side of the building came and went from the cafeteria, Vee wasn't among them.

Considering it was the day after a win, the players sitting around my table were more solemn than usual. It was our collective concern over Dennison. The most animated the discussion became was when Packard's name was mentioned. The consensus was that the NFL should fine him in addition to his three-game suspension.

The last meeting of the day was with Coach Garcia, my quarterback meeting. Since Dennison was out, it was only the two of us.

"You came through for us, Fin," he said as I took a seat. "Your instincts are good." His forehead furrowed. "Coach Pratt calls plays for a reason."

"It was a good call until it wasn't," I said. "The defense read our lineup. The backs didn't have a chance of completing the first down. Patel was open. The first down gave us time to run out the clock."

"You should know," he said, "there's talk about bringing on a third-string quarterback."

I nodded. "It makes sense. Simpson?" I asked.

"Why do you ask?"

"He knows the plays. It makes the most sense. Last I heard he was signed on to New Orleans's practice squad."

"How would you feel about being let go and re-signed?"

I shrugged. "It's part of the business, Coach. We know the routine."

Coach Garcia nodded. "How are you feeling?"

"Like I told Lacy Reynolds, I apparently blocked out the day after getting run over by multiple trucks, maybe even a few buses."

Garcia smirked. "You're good for next Sunday."

It wasn't a question, and yet I answered. "Next Sunday isn't in question. Reynolds wants me to ice and heat my shoulder over the next two days. If I'm still sore on Wednesday, I'm supposed to see her before practice."

"Keep me updated. We need you ready for Sunday."

"I will, Coach."

CHAPTER 22

Vee

Dennison was the topic of Monday morning's executive meeting. The debate centered on if he would be put on the IR and kept off the field for a four-week minimum. "It's not only the concussion," Dad said. "The neck sprain is a concern. He came down hard on his spine. His helmet hit Packard's first and then the ground."

"Have we thought any more about calling back Simpson?" I asked.

Uncle Darin lifted his eyes from the papers before him. "It's on the table, Vee."

"Are you trying to push Fin out?" Grant asked.

"This isn't about Graham," I replied. "It's about the

Coopers having depth on the bench. Heaven forbid Fin meets the same fate as Troy." Speaking the scenario filled me with dread.

"Vee is right," Aunt Rachel said. "Darin and I spent hours looking at available quarterbacks. While we could get one or two cheaper, the issue is practice and knowing the plays. Cody Simpson knows our playbook. He's familiar with our coaches, and they're familiar with him."

Uncle Darin exhaled. "His agent knows he has us over a barrel. Simpson isn't returning for the same salary we had him on before."

The entire table turned to Dad.

My father laid his hands on the table's surface and sighed. "Darin, talk to Cody's agent. Get a price and a timeline. Bring it to me. We need a backup by next Sunday." He moved his green gaze around to each member of the committee. "We have five more games before our bye. If it will make Dennison healthier for playoffs, I think he should be on the IR."

"No," Grant replied. "You want to put the first half of the season in an old man's hands."

I spun my face toward my cousin. "Excuse me. Weren't you the one who advocated for Griffin Graham?"

"As backup. As a mentor. In their short time together, the plan worked." He lifted his eyebrows. "I'm sure you saw that during your observation."

"Vee?" Dad asked.

"Troy and Fin worked out after each practice. Drew said the two would even work out on Tuesdays. I know Fin was concerned about Troy and spoke to him after the news conferences yesterday."

"How do you know that?" Grant asked.

I straightened my shoulders and used my most even tone. "He told me."

"Griffin told you?"

"Yes." I turned back to Dad. "If Dennison is on the IR, Simpson's re-signing is priceless." I tried to read his expression. "This season is on the line." My volume rose. "And we've only played one regular season game. Dennison will heal and when he does—"

"We'll have two overpaid backup quarterbacks," Uncle Darin interjected.

The ensuing discussion was quickly squelched by my father. "While I appreciate your knowledge and input in the matter" —the room quieted— "as sole owner, the decision is mine. Darin, talk to Simpson's agent immediately. Once I have the numbers, I'll talk with Royce and decide. Any further business?" When no one responded, he added, "Meeting adjourned."

As I gathered my things, Dad said, "Vee, stay for a minute."

Nodding, I set my tablet and papers on the table. As I waited for others to leave, I secured the button-lined large cuffs on my long-sleeved blouse. While it was summer, the sleeves themselves were sheer. I chose the blouse for the long cuffs, which covered my bruised wrists. Once the door was closed, Dad leaned forward. "Do you remember what I said a few weeks ago?"

Though I searched within the recesses of my mind, I shook my head. "It's been a busy first month of the season."

"I told you that you and Grant would be working together in the future. I also said that while Grant is essential in communication, he also has a good mind for the football side of the business. That is changing. Drew is very impressed with what you've learned in football operations. Yet, I stand by my word; you have the heart of the Coopers as your main concern. What do you think your grandfather would do in this situation?"

"I think he'd do everything he could to re-sign Cody Simpson."

Dad smiled. "You didn't hesitate. You didn't defer to Royce." He nodded. "I like that. Now, what if the numbers don't compute?"

I shook my head. "How much are we talking, Dad? How much is too much to give the bench some depth. Listen, I was against signing Fin, especially with the higher salary Royce insisted we offer. I can admit I was wrong. Griffin Graham is a valuable addition to the Coopers. I was also right in the fact that Fin is thirty-six, nearly thirty-seven years old. If a game is going well, let him rest and have a quarterback who is ready to jump in on day one."

"If Fin gets hurt?" Dad asked.

"We're fucked. Talk to Drew, get the O line ready to protect him under all circumstances." I fought a smile remembering Fin saying he'd been hit by big men.

My dad nodded. "As I said, Drew said you're a quick learner. Did you hear anything interesting with the earpiece?"

Would I be throwing Fin under the bus to tell Dad what he did?

Does Dad already know?

Is this a test?

"I heard Drew call a run play," I said. "While both backs were available, Fin went to the pass option."

Dad nodded. "What do you think about that? Insubordination?"

"No," I replied honestly. "I think the reason Royce was willing to pay for Griffin Graham was because he brings more to the team than a throwing arm. Fin has experience. He read the defense and determined that neither back would succeed in a first down. If that happened—we'd been stopped—we would have had to punt to Tennessee. They would have gotten the ball back. Their defense was expecting our run game. Fin read it correctly and made the right adjustment." I almost added that I told him so but stopped myself.

Dad stood, scooting back his chair. "I'm proud of you, Vee. You remind me more and more of your grandfather every day."

Something I'd buried in the overload of my recent new workload came back to me. "Grant made a comment about a change to your will. Uncle Darin told him and Lip the team was to be divided three ways."

Dad took a deep breath. "That's not completely accurate."

"Kind of accurate?" I asked.

"I never understood why my father cut Rachel out of team ownership. It's why I've always included her and Darin."

"Are you worried that I won't include Uncle Darin, Grant, and Lip?"

"Should I be?"

I met Dad's green stare. "Grant is a never-ending thorn in my side, but no. Each one of the people around this table has specific knowledge that's necessary to keep the Coopers successful. They all have a stake in the franchise."

"Don't you think that stake should be as part owners?"

I didn't honestly know how to answer.

I'd always assumed it would be me.

Dad went on, "I was thinking you would have fifty-one percent; Darin, Rachel, Grant, Phillip, and Leigh would divide thirty-nine percent."

I narrowed my gaze. "That only equals ninety percent."

"Vee, Daphne wants a stake in the team."

My stomach dropped. "Daphne?"

"I haven't met with the attorneys yet. Any changes in succession can wait until after this season."

"Daphne," I said again, "has never been the least bit interested in being a working member of the executive committee. Her biggest decision is what to wear on game day." My volume rose. "Hell, Dad, she doesn't know offense from defense."

"This is premature," Dad said, lifting his things from the table. "We'll discuss it after the Coopers win the Super Bowl."

"I would never push out family." Daphne, on the other hand, wasn't my family. She'd had over twenty years to rectify that and didn't.

He smiled. "I know that, sweetheart."

Walking back to my office, I felt the uncomfortable itch, one you couldn't scratch, regarding our conversation. It had gotten under my skin in a way I didn't fully understand. I'd never taken the time to consider why Grandpa Carroll hadn't given Rachel an equal share of the Coopers. He'd given her equal financial compensation, but the team was left completely to my father, Reid Hubbard.

I remembered Dad saying he often wished he could walk into his office and find Grandpa behind the desk to ask his father questions.

Was my grandfather misogynistic?

Did he not split the team because he didn't think his daughter was as good for the team as his son?

Was Dad having the same concerns because of my gender?

Those and more questions were swirling through my head as I made my way back to my office. I had the rest of today and tomorrow to catch up on a week's work and prepare for next week before spending Wednesday and Thursday with Drew and the offense.

"We miss you around here," Jen said as I entered her office.

"I miss you."

"I saw you on the jumbotron on Sunday. It didn't look like you were missing us."

"Oh," I said, "that reminds me. I need to speak to someone in broadcasting. I don't want to be on the jumbotron. You aren't the first person to mention that. My presence on the sidelines is no big deal."

"Too late." Jen brought me a physical copy of the *Lexington Herald*. "Look at this article, right next to the one about Troy Dennison and the win pulled off by Griffin Graham."

The title was *COOPERS' HEIRESS CALLING THE PLAYS.*

"Shit. Shit." I turned to Jen. "I'm serious. I do not want to be on the screen again. And for the record, I'm not calling plays. I'm trying to understand them." I walked toward my office. "Can you also call for lunch? I don't care what. I want to spend this afternoon locked in here, wading through emails and everything else I've missed."

"Sure thing." She shrugged. "I thought the article was kind of cool. Women are proud of you."

I let out a sigh. "Thank you. While that's nice, I don't want to take anything away from the team. They deserve the headlines."

CHAPTER 23

Vee

The number of unread messages in my inbox had decreased to a number that wouldn't send my OCD into overdrive. I'd spent the afternoon on calls and Zoom meetings with a half dozen of my stadium ops supervisors. Each meeting began with my praises, telling them how impressed I was being closer to the action. They were a dream team, and I was lucky to have them.

I'd waited for a call from Drew to discuss yesterday's game, but it hadn't come. I wasn't taking it too personally, not with the scrambling going on with Dennison's injury.

Standing, I stretched my sore neck, rolling my

head in one direction and the other. I needed caffeine or a massage. Caffeine was more easily accessible.

As I opened the door to Jen's office, on my way to pour myself another cup of coffee, I was met with a familiar blue stare. Instead of voicing my displeasure at being disturbed, my resolve crumbled when I saw how the bruise had darkened below his left eye.

"Fin."

"I was about to head out, and since I hadn't seen you around…"

I lifted my fingers to my lips and scrunched my nose. "Your eye…does it hurt?"

"Not as much as being plowed down." He lifted his duffel bag. "The trainers have some remedies in here to make everything better."

We had Jen's attention.

I opened my office door wider. "Do you have a minute to discuss the offensive plays? I wanted to talk to Drew, but time has gotten away from me, and I'm sure he's busy."

Fin's smile quirked and his chiseled chin pulled tight. "Certainly, Ms. Hubbard. I can discuss the calls of yesterday's game."

My insides twisted as Fin walked past me. Instead of his sandalwood cologne, there was a fresh, recently showered scent to him. The leather loafers, pants, and button-down from last night were gone, replaced with his casual workout attire—nylon shorts and a Coopers t-shirt. I closed the door.

As the door clicked, Fin grinned. "What plays would you like to discuss?"

"I have a list, but first, I wanted to apologize."

His smile dimmed as he took a step closer. "For what?"

His proximity was a problem, as if he sent out signals capable of scrambling my thoughts. I took a step back. "Umm, I have no excuse for what I did last night. If you want to report me to HR, I won't argue."

Fin's laugh filled the room. "I took advantage of a woman who drank too many cosmos without eating. It seems to me that I should be the one to apologize."

"Okay." That would be good.

"Okay?" He lifted his eyebrows. "I should, but I'm not going to. An apology would suggest that I was remorseful about what occurred or that I wouldn't do it again." He quirked his brow. "And neither of those scenarios are true. Given the opportunity, I'd repeat everything again right here, today, tomorrow, the next day... Are you catching on to the pattern?"

"Fin, we can't."

"You told me last night you ended things with Preston." He scrunched his nose. "It was the horse manure, wasn't it?"

I reached for my temples. "Stop."

"Oh, you don't mind the smell of horse shit."

Taking a deep breath, I stood taller. "I'm not going to discuss Preston's and my relationship with you."

"I'm just trying to figure out your reservation."

I lifted my eyebrows. "My reservation. I'm management and you're a player."

"And I'm a guy and you're a woman. I'm quite sure we fit well together. At least we did. And last night, you were sexy as hell."

Ignoring the twisting deep inside me, I tried to change the subject. Jutting my chin toward his duffel bag now lying on the floor, I asked, "What did the trainers give you to help you heal? Is it for that shiner?"

He exhaled. "The shiner is fake. It's for sympathy."

I leaned back, focusing on the swollen skin.

"I'm teasing, Vee. My face will heal. They prescribed no physical activity until Wednesday morning." He tipped his chin toward the bag. "They set me up with a shoulder wrap. I'll be attached to an electrical socket, but it alternates heat and cool automatically every twenty minutes."

"Shoulder," I said, furrowing my brow. "Is your shoulder hurt?"

"Not hurt. A bit sore."

"Shit, Fin," I said, leaning back against my desk and crossing my arms over my breasts. "What does this mean for next Sunday?"

"It means I'll be—" Fin's eyes narrowed as he focused on my crossed arms.

I looked down.

Shit.

I pulled the blouse's cuff lower toward my hand.

"Fuck, Vee." He came closer, his handsome features morphing into restrained rage.

Defensively, I moved my hands behind my back. "Stop, Fin. It's nothing."

"Bullshit," he said in a deep baritone whisper. "Let me see your fucking wrists."

Lifting my chin, I met his gaze. "No."

"I'm not leaving your office until you do."

Our face-off was merely a sign of both of our stubborn streaks. Slowly, I acquiesced, bringing both of my arms forward. The cuffs with a line of buttons covered the bruising.

Fin pushed up on the solid cuffs. "Jesus, Vee." He lifted his blue eyes to meet my gaze. "I'm sorry."

"You said you weren't."

"Not for..." He stared back down at the purple bracelets on each wrist. "I-I...I didn't mean for that to happen."

"Maybe it's a sign that whatever happened last night shouldn't be repeated."

"Is that what you want?"

Dropping my hands, I exhaled. "You didn't hurt me, Fin. I have fair skin. I always have."

He took a step back and settled into one of the

barrel chairs opposite my desk. "I've remembered a lot about you." He shook his head. "I forgot that."

A smile curled my lips. "I had too."

"I'll be more careful."

The rational part of my brain told me to end this now before it got out of hand. My body, the one that was completely turned on by Fin's dominance, had other ideas. "I liked it," I said softly.

Fin brought his eyebrows together. "I'd never hurt you."

"Not hurt. A bit sore."

His frown deepened.

"I know you won't. Or at least I think I do. Last night after you left, I revisited memories I'd locked away. Shit, Fin, I trusted you more than...or I did." Emotion bubbled into my throat. Inhaling, I turned away, willing tears not to give away my turbulent feelings.

No. I wasn't doing this.

Not today.

Not again.

I lifted my chin. "Please leave."

"Vee, we should talk."

"You should go." I kept walking until I was on the safe side of my desk, took a seat and scooted my chair in. I forced myself to look up and meet his gaze. "Now."

Fin stood. From my perspective, it was as if he physically grew. From the man in the chair, he unfolded, growing taller and wider. I lifted my chin to keep eye contact.

"Invite me to your place tonight."

Exhaling an exasperated breath, I shook my head. "No."

"Then come to my place."

"No."

He crossed his arms over his wide chest. "Vee, stop whatever game you're trying to win at this moment and listen."

Game.

"I can hear you just fine."

"We have shit to talk about."

I shook my head. "The Coopers' season is all that's important." I motioned between us. "If there was something between us, it was thrown away fourteen years ago."

"Bullshit," he said too loudly.

"Fin, keep your voice down."

His nostrils flared. "This is why we need to have this discussion away from Maker's Mark."

I pressed my lips together.

"I'll be at your building at seven."

Standing, I crossed my arms over my breasts again. "It's a public building. Knock yourself out."

He tilted his head.

"You need a key to access the residential floors," I reminded him.

"Then give me a key."

"Hell no."

Fin bent down and picked up his duffel bag. He quirked a brow. With a smirk, he said, "In case you need direction, I'll pick a keycard up at the concierge before seven. Be sure it's there." His eyebrow arched higher. "Be a good girl, or our discussion will take a different path."

I stood dumbfounded and simultaneously turned on as Fin turned and walked away without even a glance over his shoulder.

CHAPTER 24

*Nearly fourteen years ago * New Years Eve*

My pulse raced as Fin unlocked the hotel room door and pushed it inward. The din of the hallway was replaced by the hum of the heating as we stepped in to the standard room. Fin hit a switch illuminating two large lamps on each of the bedside stands. Clutching my wool coat, I turned, taking in the one king-sized bed, a TV sitting on top of a chest of drawers, two bedside stands, and a chair with an ottoman. The cold-winter Lexington skyline shimmered stories below through the uncovered window. The *click* and *scuff* of Fin sliding the chain lock into place set my nerves on full alert.

I turned back toward Fin.

My date, my boyfriend...he was incredibly handsome. I saw the way the other girls looked at him at the dance. Some leered even as they were in another guy's embrace. I marveled that after these six months, we were still together. Maybe it was because I saw more to him than just the starting quarterback. I saw the man underneath, the one who excelled at play calls and struggled with managerial economics.

I saw the man who strived to eat healthy but always treated himself to a donut the morning after a game. He partied with his teammates to not appear antisocial, but preferred secluded restaurants where he wasn't recognized or hanging out in one of our apartments. He dressed up when necessary but lived to lounge around in nylon shorts and t-shirts.

His football abilities were praiseworthy. It was the man who he was underneath who had stolen my heart. The first night we met, he saved me from some drunk teammates. When practices started, he made it clear that I was off-limits.

Fin wasn't overbearing, yet his presence was known.

That didn't cause a problem between me and the other players. If anything, it opened a door for friendships without the awkward sexual tension. To most of the team I was just Vee. After living my life as Reid Hubbard's daughter, it was a refreshing change.

Being simply Vee or Abby to Fin also made him unique. The way he looked at me, the shimmer in his blue eyes, and the way we could laugh together was all without pretense. Once again, the ability to be me, not the heiress to the Coopers, was exhilarating.

Fin's suit coat was undone, his tie gone, and his collar unbuttoned. His sapphire-blue stare radiated between his prominent brow and chiseled chin, scanning over me from my hair to my red high-heeled shoes, lingering on all the places in between.

"You're fucking gorgeous, Vee."

I swallowed and forced a smile. "We didn't need to leave the dance early."

Fin pulled off his suit coat and tossed it onto the carpeting. "Those assholes were drinking way too much. The season might be over, but I don't want to be associated with a frat party and underage drinking.

"You got me a few drinks." I grinned. "I'm not twenty-one yet."

"Only a few."

"You don't want me drunk?" I teased.

Fin came closer and opened my winter coat. His chest rose and fell with his deep breaths as he peered down at my strapless dress. With a brush of his fingers, my coat slipped from my shoulders.

"No, Vee. I want you lucid as can be and fully aware of what you're saying and doing."

I lifted my hands to his wide shoulders, pressing my hips against his muscular thighs and hips. "I know what I'm doing."

He wrapped his arms around me, finding my dress's zipper and tugged. The red satin parted in the back and slithered down my body, leaving me standing in my lace panties, bra, and red high heels surrounded by a red puddle.

"Fuck me, Vee. Every guy at that dance had his eyes on you."

A soft giggle came from my throat. "I think it was every girl who was watching you."

The loss of clothing made me shiver, sending goose bumps over my flesh.

"Cold?"

"A little," I admitted.

To my surprise, Fin unbuttoned his shirt, exposing his muscular chest, and wrapped it over my shoulders. The warm material filled my senses with Fin's signature sandalwood scent.

"There, that will help while I catch up to you."

Tugging my lower lip with my teeth, I watched with bated breath as Fin went to the king-sized bed and pulled back the covers, exposing fresh white sheets. He kicked off his shoes, unbuckled his belt, and freed the belt from its loops. His pants fell to the carpet, soon joined by his socks. Lastly, he came to me, offering me his hand. "We only need to do what you're comfortable doing."

Willingly, I laid mine in his and stepped away from the red satin puddle. I looked up. "I trust you. You've never given me a reason not to."

He led me to the bed.

"I want to finally be inside you."

Swallowing, I nodded. "I think I want that too." I climbed onto the mattress and sat on my bent legs.

Fin grinned. "It's time to lose my shirt."

Without hesitation I pulled it off my shoulders and threw it to the carpet.

"Come on, Vee. Yes or no?" He reached for the closest lamp and switched it off.

"Yes," I said, tilting my head. "Just leave the other light on, okay?"

"Fine by me. I love watching you come." Placing his fists on the side of the bed, Fin crawled in my direction. Fist, knee, knee, and then fist. His shoulders shifted as his gaze remained laser focused. Fin was a giant predator stalking his prey. The visualization twisted my core.

I was his prey. Yet, it wasn't fear coursing through my circulation but anticipation.

"I-I..." I took a breath and lifted my hand to his shoulder. "I'm not stupid, Fin. I know how this works. But..."

"But?"

"I wouldn't mind if you told me what to do, what you want."

He effortlessly unsnapped my strapless bra and tossed it on the ground, his attention on my breasts before looking up to my eyes. "You want me to be in control?"

I nodded.

All at once, I was lying on my back and Fin was over me, straddling my torso with a smile filled with promise. A giggle escaped my lips as I looked up at him.

"It's a two-way street," he said. "I like control. What do you like?"

Warmth filled my cheeks. "I like it when you go down on me."

His smile quirked as Fin shimmied down my legs, dragging my black lace panties with him until they were lost somewhere on the carpet with the rest of our clothes. With me fully nude, the only barrier to tonight's objective was Fin's boxer briefs.

"Spread your legs for me."

I lost myself to his deep baritone timbre.

"Good girl."

This was so unlike me, Maeve Hubbard. I was the person who sought control in all things. Group projects, I always volunteered to be the leader. With the football team, I took on the role of organizer of the water people. Trusting others when there was a goal at stake didn't come second nature to me. I could blame this trait on my father. He was very much a take-charge person. He'd passed that on to me, his only child.

And yet with Fin, I willingly surrendered that which was second nature.

As he buried his face between my thighs, I appreciated the amazing freedom in submission.

Free to feel.

Free to let go.

Free to fly.

The discovery was new and intriguing.

I gripped the white sheets as Fin sucked and licked my core. My pussy convulsed when he eased one and then two long fingers inside me. Panting for breath, I felt the tightening as my insides twisted, tighter and tighter. Keeping his fingers busy, his lips moved upward—my lower stomach, my stomach, up to my breasts. More licks and sucks. When his teeth joined the fray, I called out his name.

"Open your eyes."

I did as he said.

"Good girl."

His sapphire stare met mine with our noses close enough to touch. His kiss tasted like me as his tongue tangoed with mine. I wasn't sure when he'd removed his boxer briefs, but I knew by the probe and weight of his penis against my stomach, it was free.

"I want to be inside you," he said.

"I want that too."

After directing his cock to my folds, Fin reached for my wrists, lifting them above my head. The movement caused my back to arch. Again, he gave his attention to my breasts. I was so wound up by what he was doing that the jolt of his penetration caught me off guard.

Instinctively, I pulled at my wrists.

Fin didn't loosen his grip.

"Vee, are you still with me?"

Opening my eyes, I nodded, his handsome face blurry with my tears. Fin leaned down, kissing and licking each cheek before slowly moving his length and girth within me. The pain began to subside. My body relaxed. As I did, he released my wrists and all at once, I ran my fingers over the muscles in his shoulders.

The freedom to move was a gift that added pleasure to what we were doing.

The pleasure built, not as much as with his mouth, but it was there.

Fin's thrusts came faster as the muscles and tendons in his neck and shoulders strained. The changes in his facial expressions created a truly marvelous show as he came. Fin's grunts and deep guttural roar filled the air.

He collapsed his weight over me, before bending at the waist and staring down at me. "Shit, are you okay?"

A smile came to my lips. "Better than okay."

Fin smoothed my hair away from my face. "You were perfect."

Never had three words meant as much.

CHAPTER 25

Vee

Present day

Getting out of my car in the garage in my building, I continued the internal argument I had been having with myself since Fin left my office. Damn him. Damn his sexy grin and damn the kiss last night. Damn the memories. I wasn't a lovesick twenty-year-old. I was the Coopers' vice president of stadium operations and marketing and Reid Hubbard's only child.

The Coopers had more important things happening than whether Griffin Graham made me hot and bothered. Before I left Maker's Mark, the training staff released the final injury report. Troy Dennison was officially on the IR. That gave us space on the roster to bring on another quarterback. It also meant Troy couldn't practice for four weeks. In all likelihood, he wouldn't return to the playfield until after our bye, week seven.

Providing a keycard with the resident concierge was something I used to do for Preston. He asked for a permanent key, but I deflected. The key from the concierge was only good one time and only to access the resident floor. It didn't allow entry to my condominium.

During the last few hours, I'd concocted completely rational reasons for not providing a keycard for Fin.

First and foremost, a relationship between Fin and me was wrong. During the last hour, I'd gone over the HR website, and while I couldn't find a specific franchise rule that we would be violating, I felt in my soul it was a violation.

Owners and players—it was fundamentally wrong.

Second, my recent conversation with my father was nagging at the back of my thoughts. When he mentioned increased duties a few weeks ago, he asked if that would be a problem. He'd meant with Preston, as if a relationship was more of an issue for a woman than a man.

In hindsight, apparently my increased responsibilities were a problem for Preston.

The good news was that Preston was no longer a problem.

However, if in the future, Dad believed my attention was divided with Fin, that could possibly support his reasoning for dividing the Coopers in his will. Hell, he was married and so was Aunt Rachel. Owners could balance work and life.

While I understood his reasoning about our family's stake in the team, I didn't like it.

Lastly, there was Grant. If anyone was to make a deal out of Fin and me revisiting our relationship, it would be my cousin. Surely, he'd find an issue.

As with any argument, there were also counterarguments.

Allowing Fin entry into my condo didn't mean that we would get back together. He said we had shit to discuss. He was right. Lip's comment telling me to ask Fin why he didn't call came to mind. It wasn't a question I wanted to pose at Maker's Mark or on the sidelines. I could see it now. "Hey, before you run that play, why didn't you return my calls all those years ago?"

That was definitely not the way I should present it.

Speaking in private was better.

I also knew me. If I made it all the way up to my apartment without stopping on the first floor and arranging for the keycard, I knew I wouldn't come back down. I'd bury myself in my condo, make a lame excuse for dinner, and read a book or practice offensive plays.

Stepping into the elevator, I felt as if I was no closer to a decision.

As the elevator doors closed, I hesitated.

Decision made.

I'd leave it up to fate.

Yes. It was the perfect answer, just like the flip of the coin at the start of the game.

Flashing my keycard before the sensor, I hit the button for the seventh floor. If there were other people on the first floor and the elevator stopped, boom. Fate was telling me to leave the key. If there wasn't anyone and the elevator didn't stop, fate was saying no.

My breathing hitched as I watched the numbers on the screen.

The G disappeared.

The one illuminated.

Was it going to stop?

"Fuck it," I mumbled, hitting the one. Fate hadn't made the decision, I had.

The doors opened to an empty space. No one was waiting on the first floor to enter the elevator. The decision was made. I wasn't doubling back. Lifting my chin, I walked toward the resident concierge desk. The man behind the counter peered up as my shoes clipped the marble floor, my taps growing nearer.

"May I help you?" a young man with the name tag *Jace* asked.

"Yes. I'm Maeve Hubbard from number 706."

"Hello, Ms. Hubbard. It's nice to see you again."

I feigned a smile. "I'd like to request a one-time entry keycard for a guest to visit me this evening."

"Sure thing, Ms. Hubbard," the man said, reaching for a tablet and pen. "Will this guest be Mr. Clark or Mr. Hubbard?"

I blinked.

Of course he'd think that. Preston and my father were two of my most frequent visitors. "No. Today's visitor is Griffin Graham."

The concierge's lips curled. "Great game yesterday."

Pressing my lips together, I nodded. "Yes, it was."

I was about to remind Jace that we in the Vine paid for his discretion, but by the way his cheeks paled, I had the feeling he caught himself.

"I'm sorry, Ms. Hubbard. I'll have a keycard available for Mr. Graham. Do you know what time to expect him?"

"I believe close to seven."

He nodded. "I'll have it ready." He looked at his watch. "In thirty minutes."

Thirty minutes.

Shit.

"Thank you, Jace."

My pulse kicked up as I made my way back to the elevator. As it began ascending to the seventh floor, I wasn't convinced my debate was complete. I could always call back down and change my mind. I had a half hour. The hallway was empty as I made my way toward my condo.

Once inside, I looked out at Lexington's skyline. The September sky was beginning to bring on the crimsons and purples as the sun continued its descent toward the horizon. With over an hour of sunlight, I had an idea.

First, I changed out of my skirt and blouse and into a casual sundress. Yes, my wrists were visible, but Fin already knew about them. My high heels were replaced with flat sandals, and I removed the hair tie from my ponytail, brushing my long hair and allowing it to flow over my shoulders.

"This isn't a date," I said audibly to my reflection as I applied mascara and blush to my recently washed and toned face. "Not a date, but I didn't want to be the mess I'd been last night."

I brushed my teeth and applied lip gloss.

Next, I found a bottle of *Dangerous*, a bourbon-barrel-aged semi-sweet red wine from a nearby winery in Versailles, Kentucky. I opened the bottle, removed the cork, and replaced it with a wine stopper. Then I took the bottle and two glasses out onto the balcony.

Standing back, I looked at the small bistro table and shook my head.

"Shit, food." I went back to the kitchen and searched. Within the refrigerator, I found a half a block of Colby cheese, a small block of Swiss cheese, and a little wheel of Brie. I gathered some grapes, strawberries, and enough crackers to put together a small but adequate charcuterie board. As I stared at it, I realized there wasn't meat.

Since Fin and I parted ways, I'd stopped eating meat.

He could deal.

The clock on the microwave read 6:52 p.m.

I nibbled my lower lip.

What if he doesn't come?

What if he set me up just like fourteen years ago?

I took the charcuterie board out to the balcony. After placing it on the table with the wine, I lifted my face to the late summer sky and exhaled. If Fin didn't show, all this preparation was moot. We didn't have any shit to discuss or fences to mend. If Fin didn't show after he invited himself, I was done.

Removing the wine stopper, I poured red wine into one of the glasses. Pinching the stem, I swirled the red liquid and inhaled the bouquet of sweetness and fruit. I took a sip, enjoying the full-bodied and smooth texture combined with the flavors of strawberry, raspberry, cherry, and plum while allowing the slight amount of alcohol to calm my nerves.

I jumped at the echo of my doorbell.

"Shit," I mumbled. "He did come."

CHAPTER 26

Vee

Opening the door to my condo, my expression was tempered by the flood of memories and sense of betrayal. Fourteen years ago, Fin broke my heart; now he was back. The same cocky grin. The same glimmering stare. The same self-assured saunter.

Fourteen years was way too long to pick up where we left off. Lives changed in that amount of time. Ideals and aspirations morphed. People came and went. Decisions created pathways that only time could explore. I wasn't the same woman I was at twenty. Fin wasn't the same man he'd been at twenty-two.

It was time to face our younger selves.

"You made it," I said, taking a step back and allowing Fin entry.

He handed me a bottle of wine. "I come bearing gifts."

"Thank you."

Like me, Fin had also changed his clothes. No longer wearing the workout clothes from Maker's Mark, Fin was wearing low-riding faded blue jeans, a solid blue t-shirt making his eyes even more vivid, and leather loafers.

His grin widened as his gaze scanned slowly and precisely from my hair to my sandals and back. "The more casual Vee. Absolutely spectacular."

"I don't recall inviting you in last night." I gestured with my arm. "Welcome."

"Since I was inside, I guess that confirms I'm not a vampire."

"Ugh." I was in my *Twilight* phase fourteen years ago. "That black eye also confirms it. You would have healed by now."

His sharp chin remained tight as he scanned the condo. "This is really nice."

"A little larger than my college apartment."

"No roommate?"

"I've been thinking about a cat." We entered, passing my home office and stepping into the large open kitchen, dining, and living room area—one big room differentiated by cabinetry and furniture.

Fin turned, taking in the two walls of windows. "This puts my two-bedroom apartment to shame." He shrugged. "I suppose your contract has a better guarantee than mine."

I set the wine on the kitchen island. "I suppose. I'm not going to be traded anytime soon—or decide to bolt." If my words hit a target, Fin wasn't letting it show.

Walking toward the balcony door, I said, "It's a nice night. I thought we might want to sit outside."

Fin reached for my hand, spinning me back until I was facing him. My breath caught as I stared at the blue of his shirt, pulled tight across his chest. Swallowing, I lifted my chin.

His deep voice affected me more than I wanted to admit.

"I was hoping to repeat last night. One kiss."

Tugging my hand away, I feigned a smile. "You said we needed to talk about shit. Let's do that. Whatever happens after will depend on our conversation."

Fin followed me out onto the balcony where we were met by warmer temperatures and a gentle evening breeze. Tendrils of my long brown hair fluttered around my face. In the distance, beyond the skyline, the western sky was a kaleidoscope filled with fire: reds, oranges, and purples changing and glowing on the horizon. The sun was still at least a half an hour from disappearing.

"I already opened this wine, but if you want the one you brought...?"

Fin motioned toward the far chair.

Tucking the skirt of my dress around my legs, I sat.

It was only slight, but I noticed the way Fin grimaced as he took the other chair.

"Your shoulder?" I asked.

"I'm fine."

"Aren't you supposed to be icing and warming it?"

"I think I'll be good. I've gotten nothing but ice since I arrived."

Pressing my lips together, I sat taller and reached for the wine bottle. "This is a sweet red, but at the same time it's dry. It's from a winery not too far from here. I know most people associate Kentucky with the Bourbon Trail, but really, we have some amazing wineries too."

After pouring wine into both glasses, I looked up. "What?"

Fin's expression was difficult to read.

"You're rambling, Vee. That isn't like you."

"Honestly, Fin, you don't know what I'm like anymore. Don't make assumptions."

He nodded. "That's fair." He took a drink of the red liquid. "You were right. Sweet, but still has that dry bite." Setting down the glass, he met my stare. "Today in your office, I thought..." He shook his head. "Did I read you wrong?"

Tears I wasn't expecting stung my eyes. Blinking them away, I clenched my jaw. "I told you that I trusted you or that I did. That was past tense." I felt my nostrils flaring as I tried to breathe. "What happened when you left for Tennessee? I thought we had…" I picked up my napkin and covered my face.

Shit.

Standing, I went to the balcony, turning my back on Fin.

"Ignore me," I managed to say between attempts to fill my lungs with air. "This is stupid and ridiculous."

Fin didn't speak, yet from the radiating warmth on my back and the scent of sandalwood in the evening breeze, I knew he was now standing behind me.

If I leaned back only a little, I would feel the hardness of his chest. Instead, I spun and looked up. "I can't trust you. I don't."

"Fuck, Vee. You were the one who lied to me. I thought we had something, something I'd never expected. And through it all…" He took a step back and ran his left hand through his hair. "You couldn't be honest with me."

My eyebrows knitted together as I tried to make sense of what he was saying. "I never lied to you."

"You didn't tell me the truth."

My voice was raised more than I wanted, yet there was no stopping now. "Shit, Fin. I told you things I haven't told anyone else. I talked to you about my mother." Even saying the words caused my chest to ache. "I told you about my dreams. I gave you...you were my first. You fucking knew that."

There was no stopping these emotions, the crack was growing in a dam I'd had in place for too long. Tears continued as the blockade broke to smithereens, the hurt and betrayal now a raging rapid no raft could survive.

I reached for my suddenly aching temples. "I trusted you with my secrets, my thoughts, my body...I gave you everything I had, and you ghosted me. You said you'd call. You said it was separation in distance only."

"Vee." He reached for my shoulders.

"No." I screamed louder than I should. "I texted. I called." I wiped my nose on my arm. "I saw the pictures, Fin."

His forehead furrowed. "What pictures?"

"You at Tennessee. You and some spunky, big-boobed blond cheerleader. She was hanging all over you. You were smiling. Don't you dare lie to me and tell me you weren't happy. I saw them. They crushed me."

Fin took a step back and lifted his hand to his head. His bicep bulged beneath his sleeve. "Fuck, Vee."

My napkin was in shreds, yet I used what was left to wipe the tears and snot from my face. "Thank you," I said, standing taller. "Thank you for not denying it. I'd hate you more than I did that day if you tried to gaslight me."

"Shit, I'm not denying it. I don't remember who the fuck she was, but I'm not denying."

A scoff came from my throat. "I figured she was the ex-Mrs. Graham."

"No." He went back to the table and sat. "Her name was Abigail."

Blinking, I did a quick shake of my head. "Are you serious?"

"You didn't look?"

"No. You'd already hurt me enough. I lied when I said I didn't follow your career. Your personal life, I avoided."

"I met Abigail when I was at Green Bay."

"Cheerleader?" I asked with a raised eyebrow as I took the other chair.

"Public relations." Fin shook his head. "At Tennessee, there were a lot of girls. I honestly don't remember them. I wouldn't know them if they walked in here today. I know I sound like an ass, and I probably was. I used them, every one of them, for one purpose."

"What?"

"To get you out of my system."

CHAPTER 27

Fin

Vee was more than what others in the Coopers' organization saw. In this rare moment, she was broken; she was real and raw with her swollen eyes and red nose. While crimson splotches dotted her neck and decolletage, she was still beautiful. I longed to reach out, to hold her, and to beg her forgiveness.

I couldn't.

There was still more truth yet to reveal.

She stood, her arms stiffening as her palms slapped her thighs. "Bullshit." She spoke louder. "I call bullshit, Fin. Poor you. Quarterback, revered by all, suffering through hundreds of brainless Barbies. My heart breaks for you. All that sacrifice just to get *me* out of your system." Her volume rose. "I called you. I texted you. If you wanted me out of your system, you should have returned the damn calls. Told me goodbye. No, you didn't do that. You moved on as if I never existed."

"You fucking existed, Vee. Back then, I didn't want you to."

Her green eyes doubled in size.

"You want to talk about sharing?" I didn't wait for her to respond. While I tried to keep my tone even, the pain this conversation unearthed wasn't Vee's alone. "Vee, you were the first girl—the first woman—who didn't look at me like a lifelong meal ticket. I didn't have to be smart, or funny, or sexy every fucking minute we were together." I stood. "I shared shit too. I told you things I've never shared with anyone. I told you about my aspirations for professional ball. Hell, I took you to my parents' home in Bowling Green." Scoffing, I shook my head. "I bet that was something you told all your rich friends about."

Vee tilted her head. "What are you talking about?"

"Thanksgiving. You said your dad and stepmother were going to be out of town and you would be going home to an empty house."

She nodded. "Yeah, the Coopers had a game in New York."

"You didn't fucking say that. You never said a damn word about the Coopers." I inhaled, gripped the railing of Vee's balcony, and looked out over Lexington. The sky beyond was growing darker, just like my mood. "My parents' modest four-bedroom ranch was probably laughable to you."

"No." Her tone was softer as she reached out to my arm. "Fin, I loved your parents. They were so nice. Your mom taught me how to mash potatoes." She exhaled. "Not that Daphne ever cooked."

My timbre was cold. "My turn to call bullshit."

Vee's large emerald-green eyes were fixed on mine. "I-I don't understand."

"Did you enjoy slumming it?"

"I-I never—"

"Did you go back to Emma and tell her how average my family was? Did you tell her how small their home was? Did you have a good laugh?"

Tears streamed down Vee's pink cheeks. "No," she said definitively. "Why would you think I would do that?"

"I didn't, not at the time."

Vee turned, sitting back down in the chair. When I looked, her face was in her hands. She looked up. "Oh God, do your parents think that?"

Her draw was too strong to resist.

I crouched and laid my hand on her knees. "I never

told my parents. It would have broken my mom's heart. She really liked you."

"I-I don't understand why you think such horrible things about me."

Inhaling, I stood. "I told you. You weren't honest with me."

"Fin, I told you everything about me. I shared everything."

"Except?"

My one word hung in the air.

Streetlights came to life stories below, and a warm glow came from the windows of her million-dollar condominium.

Vee stood, her shoulders squared. "I told you my name. You knew I was from Lexington. You knew my love of football. You met Leigh. You knew Daphne's name. I'm sure I mentioned Dad."

"Dad. You did mention your dad, never by name."

She spun around. "I don't call him Reid. I call him Dad."

"I want you to imagine, you're starting a new team in Tennessee. A teammate you hardly know sees the picture of the girl you love in your locker, and instead of saying the normal compliments, he makes an offhanded comment about me using you to get into the NFL."

"Fin." My name was barely audible. "Shit."

"Talk about fucking blindsided."

Her hand was on my arm again. "You didn't use me. I know that."

"Because you didn't fucking trust me enough to tell me who you were, who your father was."

"I told you," she said, "a few weeks ago in the parking lot. No one on the UK team knew, except the coach." She exhaled. "I wanted to be me, not Reid Hubbard's daughter." She shook her head. "Not the Coopers' heiress. Me. I thought that was enough for you." Vee picked up her glass of wine and drained it. "Obviously, we were both wrong."

"Vee." When she didn't respond, I said, "Abby."

"Oh hell no." Vee spun my direction. "Never call me that again."

"Abigail went by Gail, not Abby."

Vee shook her head. "Don't, Fin. I don't understand. Is this" —she motioned between us— "what you wanted? Was this why you came to the Coopers? You wanted to punish me for not telling you something obvious?"

"Obvious?" I questioned. "If I meet someone from Atlanta with the last name Blank, should I immediately think of the Falcons? How about Pegula?"

"Buffalo Bills."

"Fuck, at twenty-two I hadn't spent my life around football owners. Hubbard was just a name."

"And I loved you for that." She reached for the door handle. "You hated me for it. This seems like an impasse." She kept the door open, pressing her petite frame against the glass. "Your contract is safe—unless you plan on bailing on it too."

"I wouldn't have bailed if you…"

Vee smirked, keeping her chin high. "I took you for someone who took personal accountability. Wrong again." Vee motioned through her condo. "You can go now."

"I don't want to go," I replied truthfully. "Vee." I softened my tone. "Now that the air is clear, can we try again?"

Pressing her lips together, she shook her head as her face fell forward. Her long hair created a veil separating me from her.

"Fuck." I spun a complete circle, doing my best to keep it together. "I should have returned your call. I didn't know you saw pictures."

Lifting her hands to her temples, Vee laughed. It wasn't a real laugh, not sincere. "You're sorry I saw pictures. You're not sorry I thought we had a future, and it was shattered. You didn't have the decency to talk to me, text me, shit, Facebook message me. I know communication wasn't as advanced fourteen years ago. Hell, I would have taken smoke signals." Using her palms, Vee wiped her cheeks. "Please go, Fin. Go home. Take care of your shoulder. With Troy on the IR, the Coopers need you."

"You weren't listening."

Her bloodshot stare met mine. "I heard every word."

I'd told her I loved her. The girl in the picture in my locker. I loved her, more than I'd loved anyone before or after. "Every word?"

Vee nodded. "Goodbye, Mr. Graham. We'll keep things professional, I hope."

"Things shouldn't end like this."

"It's more closure than I had before." She lifted her chin and blew through her lips. "It sucks, but it's closure."

"Think about what I said."

"Fin, if you want me to apologize for being the reason you screwed nameless women, you'll be waiting a long time."

The buzzing in my ears grew louder as I rode the elevator down to the garage. Talk about a colossal fuck-up. Coming to Lexington was a mistake. I should have retired. Once I was in my truck, I looked up at the rearview mirror and brought my fingers gingerly to my cheek. "I'm getting tired of being knocked around."

My phone buzzed.

Coach Garcia, the Coopers' quarterback coach's name was on the screen.

"Coach?" I said, answering.

"Graham, I wanted you to hear it from me. Cody Simpson re-signed with the Coopers."

I let out a sigh. "That's good."

"You're not upset?"

"Shit no. I'll be ready to run reps with him Wednesday."

"Are you taking care of your shoulder?"

I peered around the parking garage. "I just finished icing it, following doctor's orders."

"See you Wednesday."

CHAPTER 28

Vee

On Wednesday morning, I went out to the practice field as the offensive practice was about to begin. The players were entering the field in their practice jerseys. Even Troy was there, seated on the sidelines in street clothes.

"It's good to see you," I said, sitting near him.

"You too, Ms. Maeve. I'm sorry about getting hurt."

"Troy, we're sorry. The O line is sorry. You have nothing to be sorry about."

Nodding, he looked out onto the field.

I followed his line of vision. "You have nothing to be concerned about. Number-one position is yours once you're healed."

"I don't need to be out four weeks."

I scooted closer. "It's the player's cap. If you weren't on the IR, we couldn't hire Cody back."

Troy grinned. "He called me when his agent got the offer. Cody's a good guy."

I looked up in time to see Fin jogging in full gear, coming from the facility carrying his helmet. While my chest ached at seeing him, I was happy to see he was cleared to practice in full pads. That meant the trainers thought he was healed enough to play on Sunday. He glanced our way and immediately turned toward the other players.

Troy nodded toward my notes in my hand. "If you want any help with that, I'm free."

My grin returned. "Thanks, Troy. I would like that very much."

Troy was at my side during Wednesday morning and afternoon practice as well as Thursday morning practice. I'd tell him what I thought had been called and what was played. He'd either correct me or let me know I was correct.

"The players think you're pretty cool, Ms. Maeve. You're working hard and we respect that."

"Thanks," I said with a sigh. "Sometimes it's nice to hear encouragement."

"You've got it from us."

Thursday afternoon, I let Drew know I would leave practice early. My dad scheduled our flight to leave before the team's. He had plans with the CEO and controlling owner of the Broncos. Daphne was nothing but talk about the outfit she'd bought.

Sitting in the middle of the Hubbard Gulfstream, I had Drew's playbook and notes in front of me when to my surprise, Lip and Grant entered the plane. I waited until they saw me. Lip's eyes lit up. He widened his stride and made his way to the four-person seating around the table, taking the seat across from me.

"I didn't know you were coming," I said.

"It was a last-minute decision."

Grant stood at our side.

Looking around, I realized Lip and I were taking the two outer seats. My tote was in the seat to my side. "Do you want to sit?"

Grant shook his head and gestured toward the front. "I can sit over there."

"We can make room," Lip said.

"Vee, are you going to stand on the sidelines Sunday?" Grant asked.

My neck straightened. "Yes."

His head shook almost imperceptibly. If it weren't for the way his light hair moved, I might have missed it.

I lifted my tote and scooted to the side. "Grant, you're welcome to sit here, and I'll explain what I've learned."

"Jesus, Vee. I understand play calls. You'd think you'd just secured a million-dollar grant. It's not rocket science."

Inhaling, I turned my attention to my other cousin.

Lip reached across the table and took both my hands in his. Turning to Grant, he said, "Go suck up to Uncle Reid. I see him and Daphne on the tarmac."

Without another word, Grant walked away. He settled on a chair facing forward. My chair was the same direction. We were separated by a partial wall.

"Mr. Phillip and Ms. Maeve," Susan, one of our regular hosts said. "We have roughly four hours until landing. Mr. Hubbard asked for a light salad. I believe he and Mrs. Hubbard have dinner plans once we arrive."

While our flight was four hours, with the time difference, we'd only be two hours ahead when we landed.

"I'm good with a light salad," I said. "I'd love some coffee with cream."

Susan smiled. "Mr. Phillip."

"Salad is fine." He pressed his lips together. "I'll take a Woodford and ice."

"Right away."

My gaze met Lip's. "Trouble in paradise? Isn't it early for bourbon?"

"We're from Kentucky. It's never too early for bourbon." He lowered his voice. "I spoke with Leigh this morning, and it seems my favorite cousin hasn't been very forthcoming."

Inhaling, I pretended to be organizing my notes.

Lip's hand again reached for mine. "Is silence the way you want to answer? If you do that, you know my imagination will run wild."

A smile curled my lips. "You've always had a vivid imagination." I spoke softer. "I'd rather other parties don't overhear."

Lip scrunched his nose. "We'll wait until we take off. Grant will have his headphones on. I'm sure Aunt Daphne will be keeping Uncle Reid occupied."

"Oh God." I rolled my eyes. "That's why I sat back here. She never shuts up."

"Hello," Daphne called to the entire plane as she and Dad boarded. "Oh good. It looks like we're all here." She waved her hand. "Susan, dear. I'd like a rum and Diet Coke before we take off."

"Right away, Mrs. Hubbard."

Lip's and my eyes met and we both began to laugh.

It felt good to laugh. I hadn't done much of that since Fin's visit. Last night, I'd broken down and called Leigh. She was one of the few who knew Fin's and my past. Or I thought she did. I thought I did. Last night we met at the Vine Club, and I filled her in on his side of the story.

She listened without judging—part of what I loved

about my cousin. It was when I recounted what Fin said about my picture in his locker that I felt the gut punch. He'd asked me if I'd listened to every word. I had. I was able to repeat them.

At the same time, I hadn't—listened, not really.

It was Leigh who commented. *"He told you he loved you."*

"He'd told me that before."

"He's telling you now," Leigh had said.

Seeing Lip across the table from me brought Leigh's observation back. "Did Leigh tell you what he said?" I whispered.

Susan returned with Lip's bourbon and my coffee.

"She told me," he said, before swirling the barrel-shaped ice cube. "She told me about his parents' house too." He leaned closer. "That was some mean shit."

"I agree. What upsets me more is that he thought it was true. Once he learned who I was, who I hadn't told him I was, he believed I thought less of him and his parents. I'm not sure I can forgive him."

"Has he forgiven you?"

The playbook blurred before me. Swallowing back the tears, I shrugged. "Neither of us said we were sorry. Neither forgave."

Lip pressed his lips together.

We were at cruising altitude when Lip asked, "What do you want, Vee?"

"I lived fourteen years without Griffin Graham. I'd given up on a future with him."

"So, you're saying you're fine with the way you two left things?"

I shook my head. "I'm not fine."

CHAPTER 29

Vee

From the moment we arrived in Denver, my schedule was full. I accompanied my ops coordinator on the stadium inspection of Empower Field at Mile High. While Denver was ultimately responsible for the kickoff countdown, as the visiting team, we had responsibilities. Along with that, I tried to stick with Drew Pratt whenever possible.

Troy Dennison became my very helpful assistant. Maybe in all actuality, I was his. I knew deep down that I wouldn't be capable of having the discussions we were about play calling if it hadn't been for the afternoon in my office with Fin and checkers.

On the few occasions my path crossed Fin's, it felt as though he made a concerted effort to look in the other direction or avoid me. It may have been my ego talking, but if it was, it was a bruised ego.

Sunday morning, the kickoff countdown went into high gear. With the game scheduled for 4:05 p.m. Eastern time—2:05 p.m. in Denver—the four-hour countdown began at 10:05 a.m.

Lip and Grant were with Dad and Daphne in a suite. Uncle Darin and Aunt Rachel flew in on Saturday. We'd all gotten together for Sunday breakfast. I was the one who left early, to get to the field in time for the one-hundred-minute security meeting. While I wasn't involved in the meeting, that meeting was the real kickoff of activities.

As the Coopers went out on the field for the last practice, Cody Simpson made his way over to Troy. I moved away, giving them some time alone to talk. When I turned, Fin had joined their exclusive group.

Lifting my chin, I walked toward them. "Have a great game."

"Thank you, Ms. Maeve," Cody said. "Glad to be wearing the Coopers amber again."

I smiled. "Looks good on you." I met Fin's gaze. His black eye was now green and yellow. "Mr. Graham."

"Ms. Hubbard." He turned and walked onto the field.

Shit.

Denver won the coin toss.

The Coopers would receive the ball to start the game.

With my earpiece in my ear, I listened to the calls, checked my notes, and watched as the players moved on the field. Both defenses were top-notch. The first quarter ended without a score. As the second quarter began, I realized Drew's play calling was ultraconservative.

Was he worried about Fin's throwing arm?

Another four and out. Our running backs weren't making enough progress.

Denver got the ball to our forty-yard line. It was fourth and inches with a minute left in the half. I clenched my teeth as we waited for Denver's decision. Would they attempt a fifty-seven-yard field goal or try for a first down?

Their offense came back on the field and lined up.

Holding my breath, I prayed our defense would not jump early. With only two seconds left on the snap clock, Denver called a time-out. Air rushed from my lungs. Coach Brown, our defensive coordinator's voice, came through my earpiece.

The likelihood of hitting a fifty-seven-yard field goal was statistically a little over fifty percent. However, Denver's field-goal kicker had hit a sixty-two-yard field goal in game one of the season. Troy and I stood near one another as they snapped the ball.

Our defense rushed.

Denver's holder fumbled the ball.

Flag—was there a flag on the play?

Malik Johnson, one of our cornerbacks scooped up the ball and took off.

My body tensed as I watched Malik run.

"To the fifty. To the forty. To the thirty."

I balled my fist, willing Malik to stay in bounds.

"Touchdown, Lexington," came from the stadium speakers.

Turning, I looked down the bench. The entire team was on their feet, cheering their teammate. As Malik came off the field, he was greeted by back slaps and pats. There was enough time left in the first half to kick the ball to the Broncos.

Our defense held.

However, since we lost the coin toss, our defense would be back on the field as soon as the second half began. Thankfully, it was four and out for Denver to start the second half.

I listened as Drew sent his calls to Fin's helmet. Two more conservative calls. It was third and four. In my head, I was screaming, "Call a pass play." I recalled Dad telling me that I was on the sideline to observe— not micromanage and not make calls.

Next, was the call—play fifty-seven.

I looked down at my notes and shook my head.

Why the hell wasn't Drew letting Fin pass?

The ball was snapped. Fin handed it off to Dijon Ortiz, a running back. The gap closed. The stadium let out a collective groan. I looked up at the jumbotron.

Shit.

I'd been watching the wrong player. Fin had faked to Ortiz, and I totally fell for it.

Fin hadn't handed off the football; instead, he ran the ball, sliding feet first with a six-yard gain and a first down.

It took all my control not to jump up and down and cheer. Grant would have a fit if that picture was in tomorrow's *Lexington Herald*. That didn't mean I tried to subdue my smile. "Good job, Fin," I said under my breath.

Denver scored a touchdown and a field goal in the fourth quarter. Our defense was exhausted. Playing at this altitude didn't help, even with a few extra days to acclimate. With five minutes to go, we were down seven to ten. The Coopers' offense took the field.

After a fair catch, the ball was placed on the Coopers' twenty-five-yard line.

On the first play, Fin threw a thirty-yard pass to Kylon Lewis, our wide receiver. He'd been wide open. Denver's defense wasn't expecting a pass play. Fin called for no-huddle offense, hurrying our team back to the line of scrimmage. The whistles blew and flags flew. Fin had caught the defense with an illegal formation and a five-yard penalty.

We were now in Bronco territory.

I looked up at the clock. There was still a lot of time. A field goal would tie the game. A touchdown would have us ahead. Drew was telling Fin to use clock. The ground game was wearing down our backs as well as our O line.

Another third and inches, just outside the red zone. Holt, our kicker, was a pretty sure thing forty-five yards or less. Fin needed to get us closer.

This time, I watched for the fake.

It wasn't a fake. Fin handed the ball to Morgan, our fullback. The O line opened the gap. Morgan was stopped at the fifteen-yard line. It was a great run. "Good job, Morgan," I said to myself.

Drew called a time-out.

From my earpiece I heard Drew's side of the conversation with Fin. From what I could decipher, Fin wanted to go for the touchdown. While I couldn't voice my opinion, I agreed. Drew told him not to do anything heroic. We had time to settle for the field goal.

After the snap, Fin settled for a short pass to Patel. As he threw, the ball was tipped.

It sailed into the air.

Time stood still as it was narrowly missed by Denver's defensive end and hit the ground. The ball was dead. Up on the jumbotron, I saw the replay. As Fin threw, he was hit from the side and slow to get up.

Whistles blew.

Tilson, Drew, and the medical team ran onto the field.

My heart ached in my chest as I stood helplessly on the sidelines.

CHAPTER 30

Vee

The stadium applauded as Fin got to his feet and made his way to the sideline and into the blue medical tent. Through the earpiece, I heard Tilson call for Simpson to go in. My stomach dropped. Fin wouldn't want his last play of the game to be a tipped pass.

Troy looked at me.

I covered my mouth with my notes. "They're sending Cody in."

Troy pressed his lips together and turned back to the field. We lost three yards with the fumble. That made this second down and thirteen. Drew called RPO. The ball was snapped. Simpson had the ball. He stepped back, scanning, scanning. Denver's defense closed in. Simpson threw to Ramel Patel, wide receiver. Patel caught and tucked the ball at the thirty-eight-yard line. JD Downing blocked, running alongside Patel all the way to the end zone.

After the extra point, we were up fourteen to ten.

On the jumbotron, I saw Fin leave the medical tent and let out a relieved breath when I heard he was cleared to play.

Denver had three and a half minutes to get a touch-down. A field goal wouldn't be enough.

It was up to our defense now.

Despite how exhausted I believed they were, the Coopers' defense ran onto the field with vigor. Flores from our secondary hung back as the defensive line bunched up to match Denver's formation. The ball was snapped.

Denver's quarterback took a step back. He danced from foot to foot. His arm went back. It was a long pass.

Shit.

This was too fast. We couldn't let them score.

Flores came from the right field as if he were running the route. He zagged in front of the receiver and intercepted the ball. This time I didn't try to hide my excitement. All we needed to do was work the clock, and the Coopers would be 2 and 0 in the regular season.

Our defense held.

After the game, Malik Johnson stopped to talk to me. "I told you to watch the defense, Ms. Maeve. We're the stars."

My smile was wide. "You are. Great game."

Fin was only a few players behind Malik on his way to the locker room. "Good game, Fin," I said.

He turned his blue stare in my direction. There was no joy in his expression. "Congratulations, Ms. Hubbard, your team won."

It was after seven in Denver by the time we all boarded the Gulfstream. Uncle Darin and Aunt Rachel joined us on the return flight. We wouldn't get back to Lexington until after one in the morning our time.

Daphne had the back couch converted into a bed. The rest of us sat farther forward in the fuselage. It wasn't the same as flying economy, but honestly, even with the reclining chairs it wasn't that comfortable. By the time we landed, I was ready to sleep for a couple of days.

That wouldn't be possible.

Our Monday executive meeting would be at ten.

After the exciting win and the flight home, sleep should have come easily.

It didn't.

My thoughts were on Fin.

I couldn't deny how worried I was about him when he went down on the field. Or that I felt bad Drew didn't put him back in after the tipped ball. That wasn't his fault. A defender read the play and got in the way.

Mostly, I couldn't forget his expression or tone as he wished me congratulations.

I'd been right. Griffin Graham should never have signed with the Coopers.

FOUR WEEKS INTO THE SEASON, and the Coopers were undefeated. I was back at my condominium watching our home game we'd played earlier in the day. I'd gotten into the habit of recording it. Thankfully, they were showing me less during the broadcasts. There were usually one or two shots with my name on the screen.

More than anything, I wanted to hear what the national announcers were saying. Overall, Fin had the respect of the broadcasters. Many of the talking heads were retired players who had played against him. That didn't stop most of them from betting against us before the start of each game. Today's game was different. The Coopers were highly favored over the Rams.

Fin played the first three quarters. Drew took him out and put Simpson in with the Coopers up thirty-five to six. I was watching our last offensive drive in the third quarter when my phone rang.

The stupid twenty-year-old part of me wanted to

see Fin's name on the screen. Our communication of late had been limited to names. "Mr. Graham." "Ms. Hubbard."

My bubble of hope popped. It wasn't Fin's name on the screen. It was Preston's. My first instinct was to ignore his call and let it go to voicemail. And then I remembered what it felt like to be ghosted. I answered.

"Hey, Preston."

"Vee, it's good to hear your voice."

"How are you doing?" I asked.

"Fine, I guess. You?"

"Busy." It was my go-to answer.

"I watched the game. You know, before you, I didn't pay that close attention to football."

I scoffed. "The Coopers appreciate your support."

"Remember that date I promised you?"

"Preston," I said his name with a weary voice.

"Dinner? I miss you."

I shook my head, looking around my empty condominium. I didn't miss Preston. Part of me wanted to, like it was something I should be doing. Maybe I felt I owed it to him after two years. The truth was, I didn't. "Preston, thanks for calling and cheering for the Coopers."

"Vee, you look great out there on the sidelines. I should have realized how important it was to you."

"You should have," I said. "And it's okay that you didn't. Have a good life."

"I guess this is…"

"Goodbye, Preston."

Pausing the game, I walked out onto the balcony and looked up at the October sky. The lights of Lexington kept the stars at bay. Holding tightly to the railing, I thought about Preston's call. I didn't want to talk to Preston. It was Fin I wanted.

I couldn't deny it any longer.

Back inside, I picked up my phone and tried.

I typed a text message.

"HI. I AM SORRY. NOT ABOUT THE GIRLS IN TENNESSEE. I'M SORRY I NEVER TOLD YOU WHO I WAS, WHO DAD WAS. I REMEMBERED WHAT YOU SAID HAPPENED IN THE TENNESSEE LOCKER ROOM. EVERY WORD."

Tears prickled the back of my eyes as my finger hovered over the send arrow.

Twenty-year-old me was afraid to push it. She'd done it before.

Swallowing, I looked up, seeing my reflection in the window. I wasn't twenty years old. Fin could choose not to respond, but I wasn't going to miss out on a future due to my own stubbornness.

I hit send.

CHAPTER 31

Fin

I stared up at the front of the building on West Vine. The Vine Club bar was where Zane and I had drinks a few weeks ago. When some of the players wanted to get together tonight, I recommended this place. The reason for the suggestion was that I hoped the same thing would happen as what happened after the Broncos game. I hoped for the chance to run into Vee, to talk to her outside of Maker's Mark or Crystal Light. It had been three weeks since I fucked everything up with her.

Every time I saw her, I remembered the way she looked out on her balcony. I saw the tears and pain in her eyes. The things I said about my parents were needless and spiteful. The Vee I knew wouldn't have done anything like I accused her of.

What do they say?

Hindsight is twenty-twenty.

For a few minutes during our argument, I wasn't Griffin Graham, the NFL veteran quarterback. I was the twenty-two-year-old Fin who was hurt and angry. Shit, Troy was only a year older than I was when Vee and I were together. I called him a kid; the same description applied to me at that age.

What I wanted was a chance to speak with her—without the kid from fourteen years ago doing the talking. She didn't have to accept an apology, but I wanted her to hear it. Just because I didn't deserve the chance to talk to her again didn't mean I didn't want it. Today during the fourth quarter, I found myself watching her instead of the game.

She was a vision, standing farther down the sideline.

Vee said that at University of Kentucky she wanted to be Vee without being Reid Hubbard's daughter or the Coopers' heiress. Would I have treated her differently if I'd have known her association?

That question was the one that kept me awake at night because in hindsight, I think she was right. I would have been starstruck. Because watching her passion and intensity this season on the sidelines fucking made me starstruck.

Vee Hubbard was everything she tried not to be. She was Reid Hubbard's daughter and the heiress to the Coopers. Her fervor for the team and the players was on display as she intently watched every play. The way she called each player by name endeared her to the team and coaches. Vee lived and breathed for the Coopers. I was the only one who had the privilege of knowing just Vee, the water girl on Kentucky's sidelines, and I fucked it all up—again.

As I stepped inside and made my way toward the Vine Club bar, Troy waved. He and Jamir and Dijon, two of our running backs, were sitting at a high-top table beyond the archway.

"Over here," he called.

For a Sunday evening, the Vine Club was packed. Coopers jerseys and amber shirts were at nearly every table.

"Glad you got us a table," I said as I stood by the fourth chair. The one they left for me had me facing into the bar, not out to the common area where I saw Vee a few weeks ago. I considered asking someone to change seats, but I couldn't come up with a good excuse. Instead, I settled in the chair provided.

Unlike the fans around us, the four of us were dressed for a night on the town. After regularly seeing these guys in jerseys and covered with sweat, the refined editions were a nice change of pace.

Dijon spoke, his voice carrying through all the

background noise. "I made reservations down the street at the steakhouse for eight o'clock. I'm pretty sure after today, I could eat an entire cow."

A server made her way over to the table. "Can I get you a drink?" she asked me.

"I'll have a Kentucky Bourbon Barrel Ale."

"Anyone else?"

The other three men shook their heads. Their glasses were still mostly full.

"I'll be back," she said.

"What did you think about Cody's play today?" Troy asked.

I nodded. "He did well."

Troy agreed. "I'm so fucking ready to get back out there."

"It will be good to have you back. What are the trainers saying?"

"I can resume practice after next week's Cardinals game."

"Raiders?" I asked, knowing it was our last game before the bye week.

Troy lifted his glass. "I'd put money on it being you. I don't expect to see playing time until after the bye."

"But you'll be practicing?" Dijon asked.

"Damn right."

The server delivered my beer. I lifted it in the air. "Here's to having you back out there with us."

Everyone lifted their drinks and we clinked them

together. We spent the next forty minutes doing what we would do tomorrow in our offense meeting, dissecting the game play by play.

I pulled my phone from the pocket of my sports jacket. "Hey," I said. "Not to be rude. I just remembered. Zane's game is about to start. I send him a text before each game. It's good luck."

The table of men laughed. "The Vikings will need all the luck they can get for tonight's game."

"Does he send you one too?" Jamir asked.

"Every game. Even when I was in LA and never played."

Troy replied, "I bet they regretted that today."

I'd be lying if I said I hadn't thought the same thing. Throwing three touchdowns against the team that kept me on the bench felt pretty fucking fantastic. Looking down, I realized I'd missed a text message. My breath caught in my throat as I saw the name: *Vee.* I opened the message.

"HI. I AM SORRY. NOT ABOUT THE GIRLS IN TENNESSEE. I'M SORRY I NEVER TOLD YOU WHO I WAS, WHO DAD WAS. I REMEMBERED WHAT YOU SAID HAPPENED IN THE TENNESSEE LOCKER ROOM. EVERY WORD."

. . .

THE TIMESTAMP SAID she'd sent the text about twenty minutes ago. I looked around the table. "I hate to bail on you for dinner."

"Oh man..." Troy and Dijon said together.

"Something came up." I waved down our server. "I'll take the check."

"No, man," Troy said. "I got this."

"You can pay for everyone's steaks."

Dijon and Jamir nodded their approval.

After I paid for our few drinks, I bid my teammates so long, saying I'd see them all tomorrow morning. Making my way through the crowd and out of the Vine Club bar, I read Vee's text again.

"EVERY WORD?" I sent back.

HER RESPONSE CAME AT ONCE. *"EVERY ONE."*

I REPLIED. *"CAN YOU TRUST ME?"*

"I WANT TO TRY."

INSTEAD OF TEXTING, I hit the green phone icon.

It rang once, twice, three times. I was ready for it to go to voicemail when Vee answered.

"Fin."

"Come down to the first floor or call the concierge. I'm here."

"You're here? In the building?" she asked.

"I'll explain after I kiss you."

"I'll call the concierge. Don't make me wait."

"I'd be up there now if I had a damn keycard."

"I'll see you soon." The line went dead.

As I approached the resident concierge desk, I saw the young kid talking on the phone. He looked up, his eyes landing on me and a smile budding on his lips.

"...yes, Ms. Hubbard. He's here now." He nodded. "Right away. Goodbye." He looked up at me. "To confirm...your name?"

"Griffin Graham."

"And you're here to see...?"

"Maeve Hubbard."

He pushed a few buttons on a machine and pushed a keycard into it. The keycard popped out.

"This is a multi-use keycard, per Ms. Hubbard. It can only be canceled by you or her."

I took it from his grasp. "Multi-use?"

"Yes, Mr. Graham. Have a nice night."

I stared down at the card and back to the kid. "Thank you. I think the chances of a nice night have greatly improved."

CHAPTER 32

Vee

"He's here, in the building." I said aloud as I rushed into my bedroom and into my closet. The clothes I'd worn during the game, including my bra, were still lying in a pile on the floor where I'd left them. Stripping out of the leggings and Coopers t-shirt that I'd put on when I got home, I added them to the pile. Standing in my panties, I studied my options.

Something casual.

Something that doesn't say I was trying too hard.

With my pulse echoing in my ears, I pulled a green chiffon maxi dress from the hanger and tugged it over my head. The balloon sleeves cascaded down my arms.

The deep V neckline wouldn't allow a bra. While the chiffon went all the way to my ankles, the lining was a mini dress. I tugged the lining down my thighs.

Turning from side to side, I peered into the full-length mirror, seeing the skirt pitch from side to side, showing the high side slit. In the bathroom, I dabbed on deodorant and a spray of Tom Ford, Vanilla Sex Eau de Parfum.

After brushing my teeth and my hair, I added light-pink lip gloss.

My doorbell resounded throughout the condominium.

My time was up.

I took one last look in the mirror and exhaled. Touching my own wrist, I confirmed my accelerated heart rate. My purple bruises were gone. With an attempt to calm my breathing, I took deep breaths as I walked slowly toward the door. Despite my effort at calm, by the time I reached the alarm panel, I was lightheaded.

Once the alarm was disarmed, I inhaled, exhaled, and opened the door.

Words were out of reach as Fin and I looked intently at one another.

The way Fin stared at me was as if he had the power to touch me without lifting a finger. He did. Under the focus of his sapphire orbs, my core twisted and my nipples beaded beneath the chiffon. For the first time in weeks, I saw his smile with his eyes on me. His face had healed. The black eye was gone. The intensity in his eyes made him even more handsome than I remembered.

My assessment of his granite features was cut short as his large hands came to my cheeks, pulling me toward him until our lips connected. Fin was stealing not only my words but also my breath. His kiss sizzled, bruising my lips.

Without breaking our connection, he walked us into the apartment, my feet following his lead as he closed the door behind him. His strong arm surrounded me, pulling me against him, smashing my breasts against his wide chest, and uniting our hips. With his other hand, he reached behind my head, twisting and tugging my hair, causing my face to tilt farther upward. Unapologetically, his tongue sought entrance. The taste of beer and the scent of sandalwood filled my senses as every nerve in my body was ignited. Like adding accelerant to dying embers, in Fin's arms I was ablaze.

I reached up, fisting the lapels of his sports coat. Lifting myself onto my tiptoes, I pushed back, my tongue making its mark in this battle of wills. Fin spun us around until my shoulders collided with the door he'd just closed. I splayed my fingers of one hand over his rock-hard chest, feeling his heart beat in time with mine, fast and furious.

As our kiss continued, Fin reached for the skirt of the maxi dress, balling the material until he severed our connection with a scoff. "What the hell are you wearing? Does it ever end?" he asked, pulling back and scanning the dress.

My laugh joined his as I took a step back and spun a complete circle. The skirt of the maxi dress floated out.

"You're beautiful, Vee."

Taking a step closer, I lifted my fingers to his left cheek. "You're healed." My forehead furrowed. "How's your shoulder?"

"I have no physical restrictions."

My lips curled upward. "That's good to hear." I reached for his hand and tugged him into the living room. "Do you want anything?"

He took a seat on the sofa and pulled me onto his lap. "You. You're all I want."

The blue of his eyes was the color of a sun-soaked sea, sparkling with diamonds as he tucked a strand of my hair behind my ear and stared into my eyes. "I'm sorry I didn't return your calls or texts."

"I'm sorry I never told you about Dad or the Coopers."

"I watched you on the sidelines today."

How could that possibly be true?

"You're supposed to be watching the big guys, so they don't plow you over."

Fin's grin quirked. "When I wasn't on the field... when I could see you." He continued running his fingers through my hair. "Vee, Reid may own the Coopers, but you're the heart and soul. I'm glad I didn't know who you were—back then. I'm glad I got to know you without the knowledge of who your dad is. It was a privilege not given to many."

Pressing my lips together, I willed myself not to cry. "I'm happy we had that time, but I'm sad it upset you."

Fin let out a long breath, dropping his hands to the sofa. "I was a kid. You were a kid."

"We didn't think we were kids at the time."

"We didn't." He took my hand in his. "Those things I said, about my parents—"

"Fin, I never thought or said any of those things."

He pressed his lips together and nodded. "I know. I was hurt. Hurt people hurt people. It's not a good thing, but it's accurate."

Looking down at my lap, I tried to get my thoughts in order. I looked up through veiled lashes. "Do you know what I remember about that Thanksgiving?"

He shook his head.

"I remember thinking that this was what a real family must be like."

"Vee, you have a real family."

"Yes and no," I said with a shrug. "I love my father—he's done his best to be both a mom and a dad. Leigh and Lip are the siblings I never had. Other than those people, family gatherings are like a continual business meeting, except for Daphne. I doubt she can spell business." I shook my head. "I don't want to talk about my family."

"Maybe in time, I can get to meet them."

My back straightened. "Grant and Uncle Darin may be an issue."

"There's nothing on the Coopers' HR website that prohibits our fraternization."

"You checked?" I asked.

"I did."

My smile bloomed. "So did I."

Fin lifted my hand. "I loved you when I left for Tennessee, Vee. If I hadn't, I wouldn't have been as upset."

"I loved you, too."

He cupped my cheek. "Vee, I don't think I ever stopped."

The tears won.

Fin wiped the salty evidence away with his thumb. "That's not supposed to make you sad."

"It doesn't. I loved you. All those things I said a few weeks ago were true. I shared so much with you because I trusted you completely."

"And now?"

"I want to try to trust you again." I leaned forward, kissing his strong lips. When I pulled away, I asked the question he said he'd answer after a kiss. "Why were you here in the building?"

"I met some of the team for drinks downstairs in the Vine Club."

Hopping from his lap, I said, "If you'd rather…"

Fin stood. "I'm exactly where I want to be." His cheeks rose. "I think the resident concierge made a mistake."

"What mistake?"

"The keycard he gave me. He said it was a multi-use card."

Warmth crept from my neck to my cheeks. "That wasn't a mistake, Fin. It's what I told him to give you."

"I can make it to your floor anytime I want?"

I nodded.

"Aren't you worried I'll show up at all hours?"

Pushing Fin's suit coat off of his shoulders, I grinned. "That's exactly what I'm hoping."

CHAPTER 33

Vee

"Armani," I said, reading the tag of Fin's sport coat. "Nice." I folded it and laid it on one of the living room chairs.

Fin came toward me in one stride or maybe it was two. His arm again snaked around my waist, pulling my hips to his, and making my back arch to see his face. "If I take that dress off you, will I find a designer label?"

"I don't know," I answered honestly. "I buy what I like. I'm not into name brands."

"But you buy them."

"I do, if I like the style."

He took a step back and lifted my arm, spinning me

like a jewelry-box ballerina. "You're stunning in this dress. The green makes your eyes pop." He trailed his finger from my collarbone down to the deep V of the neckline, his touch tending the flames of his earlier kiss.

My breathing shallowed.

Fin's smile and deep tenor were added fuel. "I'm a fan of no bra." He quirked his eyebrows. "I don't see a zipper. How do I free you from all this material?"

"Do you think we're moving too fast?"

"No, Vee. I threw this pass fourteen years ago. It was intercepted. I finally have the ball back. It's not too fast."

I reached for his hand and led him down the hallway to my bedroom. "It goes over my head or I step out."

Fin's smile grew. "Step out. I want to watch."

Warmth blossomed on my cheeks. "You want me to strip?"

"I didn't put it like that, but yeah."

"Fin..."

He stepped back and after spotting a chair near the windows, a place I enjoyed sitting when I read, he sat down, spread his legs, and leaned back. "I'm waiting."

Oh my God.

Swallowing, I let the world beyond our bubble disappear.

It was only Fin and me.

My breathing deepened as I closed my eyes and imagined music playing. Slowly, I began to sway, lifting my arms, my hips moving from side to side. I nudged the shoulders of the dress over my shoulders, spinning, swaying. As I pulled on the cuffed sleeves, the dress continued to lower, until my breasts were exposed. Opening my eyes, I felt Fin's gaze. The intensity and air-conditioned air caused my hard nipples to morph to diamond hardness.

His baritone phrase encouraged me. "Fuck yeah."

I spun again as he'd done to me in the living room. Wiggling and swaying, I pushed the mini-dress lining over my hips. The green chiffon fell to the floor. With only my panties, I continued to sway.

The crook of his finger bid me closer.

The combined twisting in my lower stomach, flooding of my core, and heaviness of my breasts was new and old at the same time. I hadn't felt this sexy or adored since...since Fin.

A memory came back, one I'd sealed away.

I lowered myself to my hands and knees and crawled toward Fin.

"Fuck," he growled, his tone a low rumble of thunder.

I kneeled between his spread thighs. His erection was evident. Slowly, I moved my eyes upward. "How was that?"

"Fucking fantastic."

My tongue darted to my lips. "I want to suck you."

"Jesus, Vee." He offered me his hand.

We stood.

"I don't as a rule turn down a blow job. But I want my cock in your pussy before it goes in your mouth."

I reached forward, touching his erection through his pants.

Fin seized my wrist. "I'm in control, remember?"

If he were any other man I'd ever been with, that statement would have been met with a resounding *no* and possibly a slap. Fin wasn't any other man. His reminder made my stomach do flip-flops and my insides turn to molten goo.

"I remember."

His lips came down hard on mine and my body melted against him, giving myself to his pleasures because in doing so, I knew I'd be rewarded with ecstasy like I'd only known with him.

Fin scanned my bedroom. "Come here."

He led me to the window. Beyond the panes, the sky had darkened. Streetlights illuminated circles on the sidewalk below. "Turn around, Vee. Face the window."

I hesitated, not because I didn't trust him, but because it was a window.

Fin's warm breath skirted over my neck and collarbone. "No one will see you. From the outside the windows are mirrors. I looked before I entered the building. Trust me."

Facing the windows, I lifted my hands to the cool, smooth surface.

"Keep looking straight ahead and don't move those hands."

Goose bumps covered my arms and legs as Fin reached for the waistband of my panties and pulled them down. Anticipation twisted my insides as I heard the click of Fin's belt buckle and the sound of his zipper.

I gasped as his large hands seized my hips and his foot spread my legs.

Looking down, I saw his leather loafers and the hem of his pants. I craned my neck to the side, catching a glimpse of Fin's handsome face. Concentration showed in small lines near his eyes as he stared down at my bare ass.

Oh God.

His arm was moving, stroking his cock.

I longed to turn to see what he was doing.

"Tell me you're wet."

I nodded. "I am."

Fin pulled my ass toward him. His touch found my folds and his finger plunged within me.

"You're soaked, Vee. Tell me to stop."

My core clamped down on his long finger.

"Don't stop. I trust you."

Shamelessly, I moved to his rhythm, my knees bending. As his thumb found my clit, I shrieked. Electricity surged through me, detonating nerve endings and filling my circulation with endorphins.

As we became one, my back arched and a scream tore from my throat, echoing around us. His grip of my hips kept me vertical. I bit my lip as Fin filled me, pressing even deeper. The pressure and fullness felt good, better than good, better than I ever remembered.

Fin stilled.

"Fuck," he growled. "They say we build things up in our minds. We exaggerate reality in memories. It's a fucking lie. Being with you, Vee, it's better than I remember."

While I agreed, words were beyond my current capabilities. My breasts heaved as I panted heated breaths onto the glass, covering it with fog.

Fin's grip intensified as he thrust faster. The aftershocks sent seismic reverberations from my core to my toes. He fisted my hair as the twisting inside me reached a fevered pitch. His touch roamed, tweaking my hard nipples, and moving lower, swirling my clit.

His lips whispered his adoration between kisses, licks, and nips.

I was on sensory overload as my body began to quake.

We both came together.

My forehead fell to the cool glass as my knees weakened.

Fin broke our connection, spun me around and picked me up, cradling me to his wide chest. He laid me down on the bed I'd left unmade and sat on the edge of the mattress. When his eyes met mine, he teased loose tendrils of hair away from my face. "I never stopped loving you, Vee."

I ran my fingers over his shirt. Fin was still dressed and I was a nude ragdoll. "You need to even the dressed situation."

His smile curled. "I'm a fan of the power play."

"Me too. You've made it. Now let's level the playing field."

"If I get in that bed with you, we're going into overtime."

My cheeks rose. "Good."

After removing his clothes, Fin crawled into the bed at my side. Wrapping his arm around me, he pulled me close to his warm side. "Fuck, Vee. I can't believe we're here, like this."

"That...that was..." Amazing. "You're right about memories. You just blew every memory of mine away."

CHAPTER 34

Vee

Out of habit, I looked down at my watch as the football was set on our thirty-five-yard line. A smile curled my lips as we were seconds away from one o'clock. The Coopers' kickoff special team took the field. The whistle blew and Holt charged forward. The kick was high and long; our team charged down the field.

The Cardinals' player signaled for a fair catch at their nineteen-yard line.

The mixture of excitement and pride flooded my circulation.

The game was on. Our defense was up first.

With each game that I stood on the sidelines, my love for the game and dedication to the Coopers grew. While my play call notes were in my grasp, the calls coming from my earpiece were making more and more sense. Coach Brown's abbreviated call went out to Joshua Morris, our safety.

I grimaced as the Cardinals' quarterback connected downfield with their wide receiver. "He was wide open," I muttered under my breath as I scribbled notes on my list of things to discuss tomorrow with Drew and Darius Brown, the defensive coordinator.

"Come on, defense." My words weren't audible. I wasn't micromanaging. Along with seventy thousand spectators in Crystal Light Stadium, I was also a fan.

Zero to three.

Despite the opening drive pass, our defense held the Cardinals to a field goal.

It was time for our offense to take the field.

For the first time since the University of Kentucky's football season, I could admit, at least to myself, that I was in a relationship with Griffin Graham. That personal attachment couldn't be turned off at game time. Allowing Fin a place in my heart meant that there was even more than the Coopers and the Coopers' season at stake. The man I loved was out there, facing, as Fin would say, big men who wanted to knock him down.

The Coopers had the football on our twelve-yard line—not a great field position. The snap was good. Fin stepped back, reading his progressions. Jamir Bennett went wide left. Patel and Downing ran long routes.

My nerves were stretched taut as the O line gave Fin time.

His arm went back. The ball spiraled through the air, down the field. JD Downing turned as the ball arrived. It was a catch—a perfectly timed play. The decibels within Crystal Light Stadium were deafening as JD ran into the end zone.

"Yes," I scream audibly.

One play, an eighty-eight-yard touchdown.

The offense received cheers from their teammates. Fin and JD embraced, patting one another's shoulder pads. I turned back to the field, fighting my desire to keep my eyes on one man. By the third quarter, the Coopers were up by two touchdowns. With three minutes left in the third quarter, Drew sent Cody Simpson into the game.

I exhaled. Fin was on the bench where the big guys couldn't get to him.

Drew's calls were conservative. The defense was reading the room, stopping our backs and closing the gaps. With fourth and inches, Tilson sent in the punting squad.

A glance down the sidelines and I saw Fin take a seat next to Cody.

Less than one minute remained in the third when the Cardinals' quarterback threw a Hail Mary pass. The spectators took a collective gasp as the Cardinals' wide receiver caught the ball and ran into the end zone. Their extra point kick was good.

Our lead had been cut in half.

Our offense headed out to the field for the beginning of the final quarter. Simpson was benched. Fin was back out.

I was relieved and worried at the same time.

On the eighth play of the drive, the Coopers were on the Cardinals' six-yard line, second down and goal. The Coopers had kept the offense going with short completions using seven minutes of the clock.

Their defense stopped us cold on the second and third down.

The offense lined up for fourth down. Fin shouted the play. The play clock was ticking.

Four.

Three.

Two.

One.

Whistles blew.

Play clock violation was a five-yard penalty.

Drew called for the field-goal team.

From the way Fin walked off the field, I knew he

was upset. He wanted the touchdown. He'd gotten the penalty on purpose. Five yards gave Holt a better field position for his kick.

The field goal was good.

Our lead was back to ten points.

The Cardinals took the field with eight minutes to go in the game. Methodically, they moved the ball toward our end zone. Time was on our side.

Our defense was on fire.

On second down, Tyler Wood, our defensive end, broke past the offensive tackle, sacking the Cardinals' quarterback. It was a loss of nine yards. The Cardinals were now on third down and nineteen. The quarterback faked a handoff to his fullback and threw long.

Malik Johnson was covering their wide receiver. Malik turned.

An interception.

Malik was still on his feet.

"Run," I yelled.

He made it all the way to the Cardinals' thirty-two-yard line. I remembered him telling me to watch the defense, saying they were the real heroes. Malik was right. He was definitely one of today's heroes.

Five minutes to go and we were in field-goal range.

I held my breath, waiting to see which quarterback would be called. My lips curled as Fin ran onto the field. The first two calls were handoffs. We were at third and inches. Fin's handoff was a fake to Treshawn

Morgan. As Dijon Ortiz pushed Fin from behind, Fin rushed.

First down.

The crowd screamed.

"Fin. Fin. Fin." A chant erupted. The crowd was deafening.

We ended with a punt after using three minutes on the clock.

Time-out for the two-minute warning.

The Cardinals needed two scores to win or tie.

They went for it on fourth down and goal. Everyone held their breath, waiting for the referee.

Denied.

The Coopers had the ball with forty seconds left on the clock.

A sea of amber began to file out of Crystal Light Stadium.

We won.

"Great game," I said to the players and coaches as they headed into the locker room.

"Malik," I called. He turned my way. "You're right. You're a hero."

His smile grew. "Thanks, Ms. Maeve."

A smile I appreciated even more met me. "Good game, Mr. Graham."

Fin passed by closer and said in a deep whisper. "I want to kiss you right here."

Warmth filled my cheeks. "Later."

Once the team was off the field, I made my way up to the family suite. Everyone was still inside when I arrived. Scanning the suite, my attention went to Dad, Uncle Darin, and Grant beyond the glass.

"Vee," Lip called as I entered. "Damn, great game."

"Is there something going on?" I asked, tipping my head toward the three men standing behind the glass.

Lip shrugged. Before we could say more, Royce Beasley turned, seeing me. His smile grew as he arched a bushy eyebrow. "I'll take that apology now."

"Apology?"

"Griffin Graham."

"I never said you were wrong about him. I just didn't think an old man like him had it in him." I nodded. "I stand corrected on all counts." Fin definitely had it in him. I wasn't going to share that. "Troy is looking good. He'll start practicing this week."

As our conversation moved on to Troy Dennison, Dad appeared at my side, carrying a pink drink.

I narrowed my gaze. "You going to froufrou drinks now, Dad?"

He passed the glass to me. "It's for you, my daughter and the heart of the Coopers."

I took the glass, holding it by the stem. "Thanks, Dad." I took a sip of the cosmo. "I'd say there are many important parts to the Coopers. I'm happy to be one."

Uncle Darin and Grant were still in a private discussion out beyond the glass separator.

"Is there something...?" I started to ask when Leigh joined the conversation.

"Hey," she said. "Hayden and I were waiting for you to get here." She pulled me aside and lowered her voice. "I know you can't say, especially here, but...?"

I felt the warmth creep up my neck and into my cheeks. I gave her a closed-lip grin. "Things are good."

"I need details."

My gaze scanned the suite. "I'm nervous to tell these people."

"It can't affect his contract, can it?"

I shook my head. "We've both studied the Coopers' human resources website. Fin talked to his agent. Jackson Blanch wasn't thrilled about it, but he confirmed it won't affect Fin's contract."

"So, Fin's agent knows and you haven't told Uncle Reid?"

"I will." I shook my head. "Not here."

Leigh squeezed my arm. "I'd say I feel sorry for you, but I don't. You look too happy to feel sorry for."

Dad tapped me on the shoulder. "Daphne and I are flying to Vegas next Friday for Sunday's game. Let me know if you plan to go."

"I do," I replied without reservation.

Dad smiled. "Vee, I love your enthusiasm." I looked at my cousin and back to my father. "Hey, can you and I talk in the morning before the executive meeting?"

"Sure," Dad said. "I should be in the office by eight thirty."

"Thanks."

Leigh whispered after Dad walked away. "Let me know how that goes."

Inhaling, I nodded. "I will."

CHAPTER 35

Fin

"**A**re you going out with us tonight, Fin?" Troy asked. "We're celebrating that I'll be practicing tomorrow."

My hair was still wet from the shower, and I was rolling up the sleeves of my button-down shirt. "I appreciate the invite."

"There's something different about you," he said. "You're...I can't put my finger on it."

"It's a woman," JD said. "I've seen that look in Fin's eyes before. He found himself a Coopers groupie, and she's working out his frustrations."

I scoffed. "I don't have frustrations."

Everyone laughed.

"I also didn't know there were Coopers groupies."

"Every team has them." JD wiggled his eyebrows. "You knew about them in Green Bay."

"I was young and stupid in Green Bay. It's not a groupie."

Troy jumped up. "It is a woman."

"Yes," I admitted. "That's all you're getting from me. I don't kiss and tell."

"You're missing out," Troy said. "The steak was delicious at Jeff Ruby's last week. This week we're going to Tony's."

"Have a beer for me," I said as I gathered my things. "I'm getting domesticated."

"No," Troy wailed. "I thought you were my wingman."

A genuine laugh came from my chest. "See you tomorrow."

The press conference after the game was two hours ago. The Coopers were 5 and 0 without our starting quarterback. The reporters asked if I was all right with taking a second seat to Dennison. I answered them honestly, telling them that I would have a front-row seat to greatness in the making. On top of that, I was getting paid to sit in that front row. Life didn't get much better than that.

This was the third time I'd used my keycard at the

Vine. It was nice not to have to visit the concierge's desk upon each visit. I also had a leather backpack with things for tomorrow. My spending the night wasn't set, but if Vee agreed, I was prepared. Once a boy scout always a boy scout.

Getting off the elevator, I made my way to unit 706 and rang the doorbell.

I heard the beep of her security system and then the door opened to the most beautiful woman I'd ever known. "May I kiss you now?"

Vee's smile curled and her emerald-green eyes shone. "Yes."

Stepping inside the doorway, I nudged the door closed and dropped my backpack. Without warning, I scooped Vee from her feet. Her shriek and giggle filled the air and her arms wrapped around my neck.

"What are you doing?"

"I'm carrying you to the bedroom."

She swatted my shoulder. "I have food and the game's cued up and ready to play."

I continued walking through her living room, the hallway, and into her bedroom. "Spoiler alert, the Coopers won."

Setting her feet on the bedroom floor, I reached for the hem of the soft Coopers sweatshirt she was wearing and pulled it over her head. My smile grew. "No bra."

Vee shook her head. "I'm not letting you have the power play." She came closer, unbuttoning the front of my shirt. She'd release one button, lean in and kiss my chest. Another button, her green eyes daring me to stop her, another kiss. The pattern continued, lower and lower.

I stopped her hand when she reached for my belt. "No. My turn."

Reaching for the waist of her blue jean capris, I undid the button and lowered the zipper. "Those need to come off."

Vee nodded, shimmying out of the capris.

All that was left was her white lace panties.

"Now, my turn," she said. First, she unbuckled my belt. Next, she did as I had and unfastened my blue jeans and lowered the zipper. "Sit," she commanded, tipping her head toward the bed. When I did, she removed one of my leather loafers and then the other. She rolled each sock down and off my feet. "Now. The blue jeans need to come off."

I obliged, pushing my jeans down and kicking them off. "Ms. Hubbard, is the playing field to your liking?"

Vee scanned me up and down, walking around me, she dragged her finger over my skin as she circled me once and then twice. When she stopped in front of me, Vee nodded. "I approve."

Her shriek filled the air as I once again scooped her from the floor and dropped her on the soft mattress. "Fin."

"My turn," I said, stalking toward her, starting at the foot of the bed—fist, knee, fist, knee.

Vee's eyes opened wide and her cheeks were raised as she watched me. Vee Hubbard wasn't a frightened deer watching an approaching predator. No, there was a keen cleverness to her stare and a smirk on her sexy lips. I got the feeling that instead of being prey, Vee had set a trap, and I'd willingly fallen head over heels.

We greedily removed one another's remaining clothes.

I scooted up to the headboard and crooked my finger. "Come here."

"I'm here."

"Here." I bid her closer.

My erect cock rested against my stomach as Vee scooted closer. The way her pink tongue darted out to her pouty lips was almost my undoing. I encouraged her to straddle my lap with my cock between us.

Vee rested her hands on my shoulders. "You want me on top?"

I sighed with a grin. "I've worked hard today. I thought you might be up for the hard part."

Vee giggled. "You're up and hard." She encircled my cock with her hands, moving them up and down.

I stiffened as she leaned forward, taking the tip

between her lips and swirling it with her tongue. "Fuck," I growled.

Lifting her hips, Vee positioned my cock between her folds and began moving down.

"Fi-nnn."

Her lips formed the perfect 'o.'

Vee's back arched, pushing her breasts toward my lips as her warm, moist pussy sheathed me in a tight satin glove. She moved her hands back to my shoulders as Vee flexed her knees, lifting and lowering herself.

I was mesmerized by her ever-changing expressions.

Sexy and alluring, her lips moved and her eyelids fluttered. Her emerald eyes grew darker.

I leaned forward, sucking one nipple and then the other. The room filled with both of our noises, moans and whimpers, groans and hums. Vee's tempo increased. Her fingernails pressed into my skin. Her orgasm built as her body tightened, strangling my cock as her arms and legs began to quake.

Reaching for her hips, I took over, pulling her up and pushing her down. My balls drew tight. Fireworks exploded behind my eyelids as I found my own release. Vee collapsed onto my chest, our bodies still connected.

When she pushed herself up, her beautiful face

with the loveliest smile filled my vision. "It is more work on that side."

She giggled as I rolled us.

Vee's long hair fanned over the pillow and around her face as she stared up at me. "I'm so happy."

It was a simple statement, yet I knew the feeling. Because, for the first time that I could remember, I was too. I was happy. I'd found an unexpected home with the Coopers, and more importantly, Vee and I made our way back to one another.

I teased a rogue tendril of her hair away from her face. "Me too. Did you mention food?"

Vee shook her head with a scoff. "I did, but some brute picked me up and whisked me away to the bedroom."

"In that brute's defense, he spent every minute he could watching you on the sidelines, seeing how damn sexy you were, and he wasn't able to wrap you in his arms or kiss you on the fifty-yard line."

Moving, I broke our connection.

Vee pressed her lips together. "I don't think I'm worried, but should I be?"

I rolled to her side, holding my head with my fist, my elbow on the pillow. "About what?"

"The hundreds of women you were forced to screw to get me out of your head."

My smile quirked. "Not hundreds."

"Still, should we be using a condom? I have the

insert. I'm not talking about pregnancy. I'm talking about STDs."

"I'm clean."

She lifted an eyebrow. "Hundreds."

Puckering my lips, I kissed her nose. "Not hundreds. And for the record, I never got you out of my head."

CHAPTER 36

Vee

I woke to Fin's lips peppering kisses on my shoulder, while his large hands roamed over my stomach and hips. "Morning," I said sleepily, rolling toward him and palming his scruffy cheeks before giving him a kiss. "I could get used to this."

"I could too."

Sitting up, I looked at the clock on my dresser. "Six thirty. Do you always wake this early?"

"Only when I want to make the most of my time."

Lying back on the pillow, I hummed. "What did you have in mind?"

Fin lifted his head to his fist, his elbow on the

pillow. "You should come over to my place. I mean, it's not as nice as here and about half the size."

"You're really selling it. Where is it?"

"The complex is called Fifteen 51. It's north off of 64."

"Those are nice. What made you decide to live there?" I asked.

"JD told me about it." Fin rolled onto his back and looked up at the ceiling. "I've been moving my whole life." He turned his eyes, meeting mine. "I've learned it's easier to just rent everything, the apartment and the furniture. There are companies that supply the rest, kitchen shit, towels, and bedding. It makes it easier to pick up and move again."

The sheet and blanket moved as I lifted my head and laid my hand on Fin's chest. As my fingers swirled his fine chest hair, I looked into his eyes, feeling a tug in my chest. "That must be difficult."

He shrugged. "It's part of the life I chose."

"I don't want to think about you moving away from here."

His smile returned. "I suppose that's up to you."

"Dad, but I can try to influence him." I arched my eyebrow. "Is that why you're here in my bed? Are you here to influence me?"

I giggled as Fin rolled us, me landing on my back with him over me.

"Yes." His lips came to mine, strong and possessive.

My whimper filled the air as his erection probed my leg. I pulled back toward the pillow, gasping for air as my cheeks rose. "It's definitely working."

Time got away from us as we came together. Morning sex with Fin was slower in a good way. Our hands roamed over one another as if claiming the other as our own. When we both found our release, we lay in bed.

With Fin's arm around me, I laid my head on his hard shoulder. "I'm going to tell Dad about us," I said.

"You're ready for that?"

I nodded. "You were right. You should get to meet my dysfunctional family."

"I've met a lot of them."

"As a quarterback in business meetings. I'd like you to get to know them as people and them to know you as my significant other."

Fin's lips quirked. "Is that like a boyfriend?"

"Sorta, but you're definitely not a boy and manfriend sounds funny."

"Telling your dad makes us official."

I sat up, looking at Fin's handsome face. "If you don't want me to tell him…"

Fin's finger came to my lips. "Vee, I want to shout that you're mine from the broadcast booth. I didn't want to rush you."

"Leigh and Lip know. Of course, they knew about

you before. I told Leigh that you informed Jackson Blanch—"

"Only," he interrupted, "for legal reasons."

"I know. But it doesn't seem right for Jackson to know about us and not my dad."

His palm cupped my cheek. "If you're good telling him, I'm good." Lifting his head, Fin kissed my lips. "I should shower."

"What a coincidence, I need to do the same."

By the time my hair was dry, I was dressed, and my makeup was done. I walked out into the living room. Fin was dressed in workout clothes, his nylon shorts hanging from his hips, and standing in front of the stove.

"Are you cooking?"

"I found eggs," he said, turning my way. "You're out of bacon."

A smile curled my lips. "I don't eat bacon."

"I do. You need to add it to your shopping list."

"Okay," I replied, getting close. The savory aroma came from chopped vegetables sautéing in one frying pan. There were freshly scrambled eggs in another and a bag of Swiss cheese on the counter. "Damn, that smells and looks delicious. I usually just have a cup of coffee."

His sexy smile quirked. "Haven't you heard, breakfast is the most important meal of the day?"

"I need to hurry. Dad said he'd be in by eight thirty. I want to talk to him before the executive meeting."

Fin folded the vegetables into the scrambled eggs and sprinkled the mixture with Swiss cheese. "Grab two plates and breakfast is served."

It was after eight by the time we made our way to the elevator.

We stole one last kiss. "See you tonight?" he asked.

"My place or yours?"

"I'll text you the address. You don't need a special card to access my apartment."

My perpetual smile felt as though it couldn't go away.

"See you, Ms. Hubbard," Fin said as he exited the elevator on the first floor.

I continued down to the garage. Once I was on my way, I called Jen. She answered on the first ring.

"Hi," I said, "are you at Maker's Mark?"

"I am. Do you need anything?"

"I was checking to see if you needed me. I'm on my way, but I'm going to stop by my dad's office before going to mine."

"You have emails you probably want to see before the executive meeting," she said. "Oh, and Mr. Darin Marsh called for you about five minutes ago. I told him you weren't in yet."

"Uncle Darin? I wonder what he wanted."

"He didn't say."

"I'll give him a call, and I'll be in after I talk with Dad."

"Sounds good," Jen said.

I disconnected the line and spoke to my car. "Make phone call. Call Uncle Darin."

"Calling Uncle Darin," the car replied.

His line rang and rang. After the fourth or fifth ring, the call went to his voice mail. I spoke. "Uncle Darin, Jen said you called. I should be to Maker's Mark in fifteen minutes or less."

My GPS routed me through city streets, avoiding the major interstates. The rest of the drive, I spent rehearsing how I would tell Dad my news. I was wrestling with blurting it out or easing into it. By the time I walked into Maker's Mark, I was pretty sure blurting was what would happen.

"Ms. Hubbard," Tricia, one of the front receptionists, said.

"Good morning, Tricia."

"Maeve, you're wanted in Mr. Hubbard's office."

I stood straighter. "I was planning on going there."

"They're waiting for you."

My forehead furrowed. "Who is?"

She shook her head. "I don't know for sure."

"Okay, I'm on my way."

My heart thumped in my chest as I made my way to the complex of executive offices. All I could think was that whoever was waiting wanted to confront me about me and Fin.

Who knows?

Did Lip or Leigh let it slip?

Why were they making a big deal out of this?

I clenched my teeth at the sight of Grant. Of course, he'd make more out of me and Fin than necessary.

Stepping into Dad's office suite, I was caught short by the sight of everyone on the executive committee. They all turned to me.

"Is this..." I began to say when I realized who was the only person missing.

"Vee," Aunt Rachel said, with tears in her eyes.

"What's going on?" I managed to say as a lump formed in my throat. "Where's Dad?"

"Vee," Uncle Darin said. His eyes were also red. "There was an accident this morning on 64."

"An accident?" It wasn't making sense.

"A semi-truck..." Grant said.

"Vee," Aunt Rachel said, reaching for my hand. "Reid was pronounced dead at the scene."

I shook my head. "No. No. There's a mistake."

"We need to talk," Uncle Darin said. "Reid was in the middle of changing his will. He hadn't completed the change yet, but he was going to."

Gripping the back of a chair, I willed my knees to keep standing. The room was spinning, I couldn't focus. "What are you saying?"

"Reid didn't want the Coopers to go one hundred percent to you."

My neck straightened. "My father is gone, and you're talking about the Coopers?"

"As his will stands, you're now the owner and CEO. What do you plan on doing?"

"I'm not doing anything until I see my dad."

THANK YOU FOR READING INTERCEPTED. I hope you'll continue *The Coopers* with RUSHED, coming April 6, 2025. *The Coopers* is a four-book series following Maeve "Vee" Hubbard, Griffin "Fin" Graham, and the Lexington Coopers. SACKED and SCORED will conclude *The Coopers* series.

STAND-ALONE DARK PSYCHOLOGICAL THRILLER

RISING WATERS
June 2026

THE COOPERS:

INTERCEPTED
February 2026

RUSHED
April 2026

SACKED
July 2026

SCORED
September 2026

STANDALONE ROMANTIC THRILLER:

FEAR OF FLAMES
October 2025

STANDALONE ROMANTIC SUSPENSE:

DEFENDING LOVE

June 2025

BRUTAL VOWS:

NOW AND FOREVER

May 2024

TILL DEATH DO US PART

June 2024

BOUND BY A PROMISE

October 2024

QUEENS AND MONSTERS

January 2025

TO HAVE AND TO HOLD

March 2025

NAUGHTY AND NICE - A Brutal Vows Holiday Novella

November 2025

SINCLAIR DUET:

REMEMBERING PASSION

September 2023

REKINDLING DESIRE

October 2023

ROYAL REFLECTIONS SERIES:

RUTHLESS REIGN

November 2022

RESILIENT REIGN

January 2023

RAVISHING REIGN

April 2023

RELEVANT REIGN

June 2023

SIN SERIES:

RED SIN

October 2021

GREEN ENVY

January 2022

GOLD LUST

April 2022

BLACK KNIGHT

June 2022

STAND-ALONE ROMANTIC SUSPENSE:

LIGHT DARK

Republished 2024

Previously: INTO THE LIGHT and AWAY FROM
THE DARK

SILVER LINING

October 2022

KINGDOM COME

November 2021

DEVIL'S SERIES (Duet):

DEVIL'S DEAL

May 2021

ANGEL'S PROMISE

June 2021

———

SPARROW WEBS

WEB OF SIN:

SECRETS

October 2018

LIES

December 2018

PROMISES

January 2019

TANGLED WEB:

TWISTED

May 2019

OBSESSED

July 2019

BOUND

August 2019

WEB OF DESIRE:

SPARK

Jan. 14, 2020

FLAME

February 25, 2020

ASHES

April 7, 2020

DANGEROUS WEB:

Prequel: "Danger's First Kiss"

DUSK

November 2020

DARK

January 2021

DAWN

February 2021

THE INFIDELITY SERIES:

BETRAYAL

Book #1

October 2015

CUNNING

Book #2

January 2016

DECEPTION

Book #3

May 2016

ENTRAPMENT

Book #4

September 2016

FIDELITY

Book #5

January 2017

THE CONSEQUENCES SERIES:

CONSEQUENCES

(Book #1)

August 2011

TRUTH

(Book #2)

October 2012

CONVICTED

(Book #3)

October 2013

REVEALED

(Book #4)

Previously titled: Behind His Eyes Convicted: The Missing
Years

June 2014

BEYOND THE CONSEQUENCES

(Book #5)

January 2015

RIPPLES (Consequences stand-alone)

October 2017

CONSEQUENCES COMPANION READS:

BEHIND HIS EYES-CONSEQUENCES

January 2014

BEHIND HIS EYES-TRUTH

March 2014

STAND ALONE MAFIA THRILLER:

PRICE OF HONOR

2016

TALES FROM THE DARK SIDE SERIES:

INSIDIOUS

(All books in this series are stand-alone erotic thrillers)

Released October 2014

ALEATHA'S LIGHTER ONES:

PLUS ONE

Stand-alone fun, sexy romance

May 2017

ANOTHER ONE

Stand-alone fun, sexy romance

May 2018

ONE NIGHT

Stand-alone, sexy contemporary romance

September 2017

A SECRET ONE

Prequel to MY ALWAYS ONE

April 2018

MY ALWAYS ONE

Stand-Alone, sexy friends to lovers contemporary romance

July 2021

*QUINTESSENTIALLY THE ONE

Stand-alone, small-town, second-chance, secret baby contemporary romance

July 2022

*ONE KISS

Stand-alone, small-town, best friend's sister, grump/sunshine contemporary romance.

July 2023

*ONE STRING

Second-chance, enemies-to-lovers, fake-date, little-sister's-best-friend, forbidden, stand-alone contemporary romance

July 2024

*All Riverbend interconnected stories

WHAT TO DO NOW

Visit Aleatha's store to purchase e-books, signed books, and store exclusive items.

LEND IT: Did you enjoy *INTERCEPTED*? Do you have a friend who'd enjoy *INTERCEPTED*? *INTERCEPTED* may be lent one time. Sharing is caring!

RECOMMEND IT: Do you have multiple friends who'd enjoy my dark romance with twists and turns and an all new sexy and infuriating anti-hero? Tell them about it! Call, text, post, tweet...your recommendation is the nicest gift you can give to an author!

REVIEW IT: Tell the world. Please go to the retailer where you purchased this book, as well as Goodreads, and write a review. Please share your thoughts about *INTERCEPTED* on:

*Amazon, *INTERCEPTED* Customer Reviews

*Barnes & Noble, *INTERCEPTED*, Customer Reviews

*Apple Books, *INTERCEPTED* Customer Reviews

* BookBub, *INTERCEPTED* Customer Reviews

*Goodreads.com/Aleatha Romig

ABOUT THE AUTHOR

Visit Aleatha's store to purchase e-books, signed books, and store exclusive items.

Aleatha Romig is a New York Times, Wall Street Journal, and USA Today bestselling author who lives in Indiana, USA. She has raised three children with her high school sweetheart and husband of over thirty years. Before she became a full-time author, she worked days as a dental hygienist and spent her nights writing. Now, when she's not imagining mind-blowing twists and turns, she likes to spend her time with her family and friends. Her other pastimes include reading and creating heroes/anti-heroes who haunt your dreams!

Aleatha impresses with her versatility in writing. She released her first novel, CONSEQUENCES, in August of 2011. CONSEQUENCES, a dark romance, became a bestselling series with five novels and two companions released from 2011 through 2015. The compelling and epic story of Anthony and Claire Rawlings has graced more than a million e-readers. Her first stand-alone smart, sexy thriller INSIDIOUS was next. Then

Aleatha released the five-novel INFIDELITY series, a romantic suspense saga, that took the reading world by storm, the final book landing on three of the top best-seller lists. She ventured into traditional publishing with Thomas and Mercer. Her books INTO THE LIGHT and AWAY FROM THE DARK were published through this mystery/thriller publisher in 2016.

In the spring of 2017, Aleatha again ventured into a different genre with her first fun and sexy stand-alone romantic comedy with the USA Today bestseller PLUS ONE. She continued the "Ones" series with additional standalones, ONE NIGHT, ANOTHER ONE, MY ALWAYS ONE, QUINTESSENTIALLY THE ONE, ONE KISS, and ONE STRING.

If you like fun, sexy, novellas that make your heart pound, try her "Indulgence series" with UNCONVEN-TIONAL. UNEXPECTED, UNFORGETTABLE, and UNDENIABLE.

In 2018 Aleatha returned to her dark romance roots with a dive into the Chicago Mafia with SPARROW WEBS. And continued with the mafia romance DEVIL'S DUET, and most recently her Brutal Vows series.

Returning to psychological thrillers, Aleatha released FEAR OF FLAMES and RISING WATERS.

Her love of the Indianapolis Colts shines in her football dynasty romance series, The Coopers.

You may find all Aleatha's titles on her website.

Aleatha is a member of PEN America. She is represented by SBR Media and Dani Sanchez with Wildfire Marketing.

facebook.com/aleatharomig

instagram.com/aleatharomig